# Magnificent Tales of Doomed Kingdoms

## RUPENDRA DHILLON

ELDER OWL PRESS INC.

Elder Owl Press Inc.
385 Bishopsgate Road, Brantford, Ontario N3R 0B8.



ISBN 978-1-7387300-1-8 (paperback)
ISBN 978-1-7387300-0-1 (ebook)

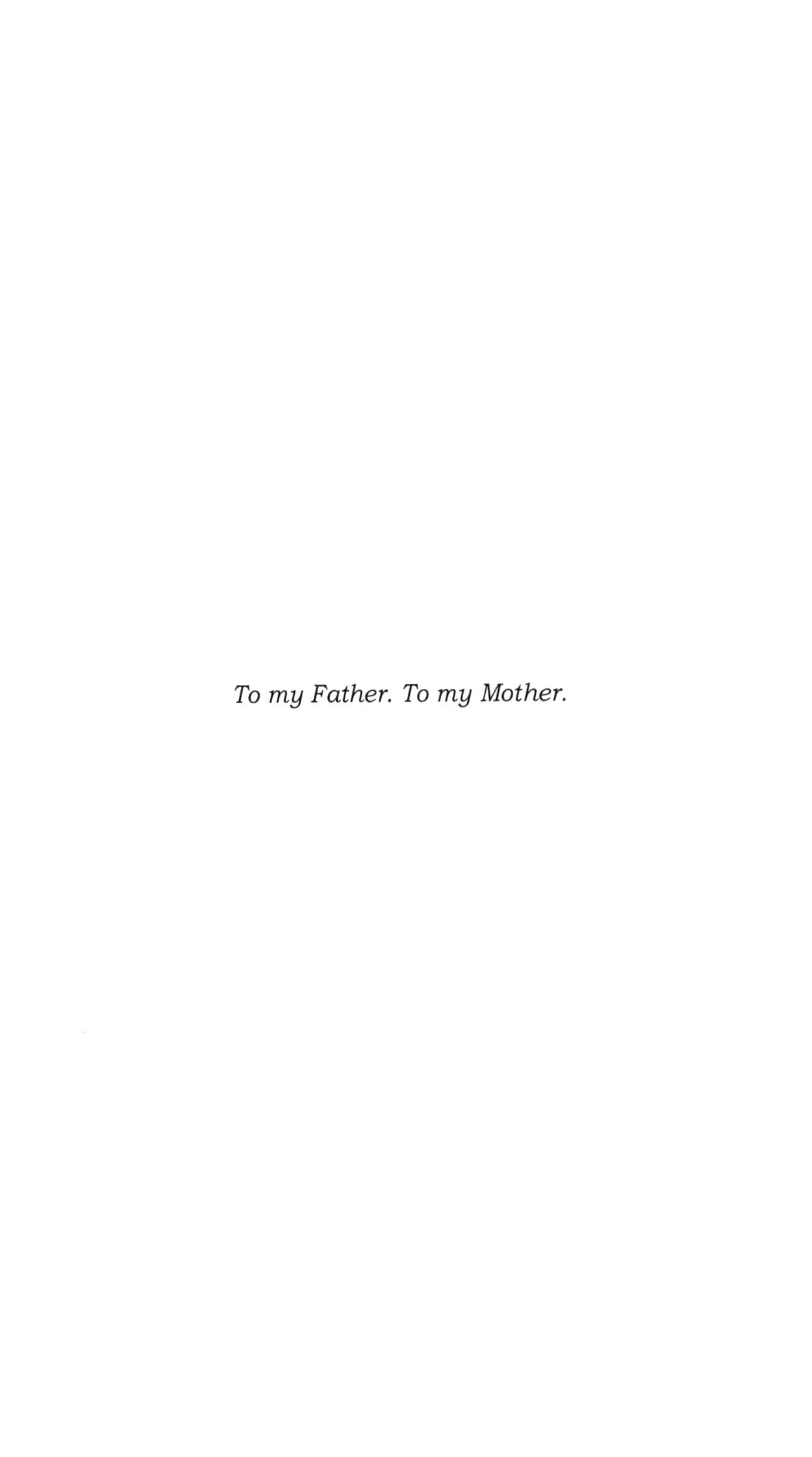

*To my Father. To my Mother.*

# A HUMBLE REQUEST

If you like the stories presented in this book, I request you to kindly leave a review for this book on Amazon. Your review would not only help to get the book noticed by other buyers but will also help them make an informed decision about buying the book.

# CONTENTS

## Disclaimer

*All characters and locations appearing in this work are fictitious. Any resemblance to real persons, living or dead, is purely coincidental. Any resemblance to real locations past or present, is purely coincidental.*

## Quick Overview of the feudal hierarchy

I believe stories in this book would be easier to understand if the reader has a basic understanding of how landed titles were organized in a feudal hierarchy. I would also try to establish the size of these land holdings as I imagined them in my mind. Note that these sizes were not set in stone. The goal here, is not about being historically accurate but to provide a quick guide to the reader. Also, reading this section is not required but recommended for better immersion.

In the feudal system all land holdings were arranged in a hierarchical manner – from large to small. Rulers in many different cultures had to contend with the challenge of assigning ownership and rights to different sizes of holdings of lands and most used a similar system. As a result, land holdings were categorized according to their size. At the smallest level there would be something referred to by some cultures as a Barony, managed by a Baron or a Baroness. Depending on the size of the Barony, it could be split into about ten to twenty fiefs, with each fief assigned to a knight or person at a similar level (in other cultures) to oversee as well as to provide revenue and military service to the

Baron. The size of a fief could be anywhere from a few hundred acres (in the range of a Square Kilometer) up to a thousand or so acres (in the range of Four to Five Square Kilometers). Given this you can imagine a Barony could range from the size of a small (Ten to Twenty Square Kilometers) town to a medium sized (Eighty to Hundred Square Kilometers) city. Each Barony would generally specialize in something somewhat like modern cities. Some would be major centers of trade, some would be places where thousands would visit to worship, some centers of production from steel to ships and then some others might mostly have defensive fortifications. Moreover, the geographical landscape of the area had a strong influence on what sort of structures would develop there over time.

When we combine multiple Baronies together, we get a county, managed in turn by a Count or a Countess. All the Barons or Baronesses in a county would be considered as Vassals of the Count or Countess and would provide services to their ruler or Leige. These services would also vary depending on the specialization of a Barony. The variation in the size of Baronies also caused huge variation in the size of the Counties. When compared to today's land units, Counties would range in size of multiple small towns to a grouping of a couple of cities and all the land between them.

The next level above a county would a Duchy. As you might have guessed, this is a collection of counties and were of a significant size. They were ruled over by a Duke or a Duchess – a ruler who was considered hierarchically second to the title of a King or a Queen (in the Western European Cultures). All Counts and Countess for the counties inside the Duchy were considered the vassals of the ruler of the Duchy. There were also cases where a ruler could rule multiple Duchies and, in that case, they were generally called Grand Duke or Grand Duchess. Depending on their size, a Duchy might be comparable to a state or a province in most modern countries. However, historically, around various parts of the world, various land holdings at the same hierarchical level as a Duchy of various sizes were carved out based on various factors such as population, financial and trade value, culture, geography, political alignments, etc.

The next level up is probably the most

recognizable to most people. It would be a Kingdom and was ruled by a King or a Queen. A kingdom would be a collection of various Duchies as well as any other lands that the rulers of the Kingdom would reserve for themselves. The easiest analogy of a Kingdom would be a Country by today's standards. However, that said, it was common for many Grand Dukes to declare the lands they controlled as Kingdoms and themselves as Kings and Queens of those lands. Since then, many of such smaller kingdoms have been combined into bigger administrative units that we know as Countries today. Hence it is worth remembering that a historically a Kingdom could also be significantly smaller than the current countries we see today.

There is one more level above a King or a Queen in the feudal system and that was of an Emperor or an Empress. This is a person who had as their vassals Kings and Queens of various Kingdoms. As you can imagine, Empires such as The Arabian Empire, The Byzantine Empire, The Chinese Empire, The Indian Empire, The Mongol Empire, The Persian Empire, etc. spanned many Kingdoms and vast stretches of globe. Today, we don't find a similar analogy to an empire, but it is not too difficult to imagine the vast scales of governance, martial and administrative control needed to bring up and control such regions.

Although the names and the number of administrative titles varied across cultures and regions around the globe, it is the above-described structure and titles that are used and thought of while writing these stories. Below I will describe these titles again and what they are called across various cultures.

| Western European | Indian | Tibetan |
| --- | --- | --- |
| Baron | Dampati/Dampatni | |
| Count/Countess | Thakur/Thakurani | Ngapo |
| Duke/Duchess | Raja/Rani | Thupo |
| King/Queen | Maharaja/Maharani | Gyalpo |
| Emperor/Empress | Samrat/Samrathni | Tsenpo |

I hope that this understanding enables you to imagine the scale of the rise and fall of the characters described in the stories that follow and achieve a greater level of immersion.

Happy reading. ■

# ESCAPE

In the great kingdom Tomara, everything was perfect – or at least close to perfect. Rajah Virbhan had a loving wife, mother, a son and two daughters who he loved with his life. Given his high prestige, two Maharajahs had already asked for his daughters to be betrothed to their heirs. Virbhan considered his wife, Gauridevi, as his best friend. Gauridevi, with her exceptional diplomatic skills took care of the kingdom when the king was away, occasionally provided Virbhan with bits of wisdom and ensured that the court decorum matched and added to its high prestige.

Business on the silk trade route was booming. Scholars were inventing new ways of doing things by applying discoveries and knowledge gained in mathematics from kingdoms of Arabia and China. Schools in the kingdom of Tomara were given the status of great universities and the brightest students from across the world would compete to get admission in them. Virbhan's just attitude and high personal combat skill had slowly won him the - *very hard to gain* - respect from jungle brigands and slowly converted them into his own paid personal army by instilling a code of honor amongst them. They were his expert scouts, trackers and rangers that would not only protect the outlands of any illegal activity but also worked as his spies to track movement of enemy activity. It seemed lady luck was smiling on the kingdom of Tomara.

The Rajah had led a difficult life to get where he was. He had started his journey as a Thakur and slowly worked his way up to become the Rajah. This required him to take over the lands from his liege's favorite vassals followed by defeating his liege, gaining independence, and acquiring all his lands as well.

His councilors usually told him that no one would call him as someone who didn't do enough for his family if he would retire now. He had done enough and although he could do more, he didn't need to. Virbhan considered his councilors' advice multiple times but couldn't bring himself to find a good enough reason to retire. He was not even forty yet – although that said, some of his childhood friends had already passed away in the numerous duels and wars around him as he was growing up.

Virbhan had seen the dangers of battle firsthand and the only thing that he felt still needs to be completed is to ensure his son, Rajputra, now fifteen, understands how to rule, defend, and possibly grow his kingdom. This, however, was easier said than done. Like many other kings who had been blessed by a single son, Virbhan understood both the advantages and the dangers of such a situation. Having a single son allowed the whole kingdom to be passed as-is to the son at the time of succession instead of the kingdom splitting in small petty kingdoms between many sons and degenerating to anonymity. This blessing, however, was also similar to having all your eggs in the same basket. Virbhan had to spend a considerable sum on his spy network to ensure any plots to kill his only son and heir were found and ended as soon as possible. He was glad that he could appoint his very skilled mother as the grand spymaster and she could, working with his wife, ensure that there are no problems for the family. He had even betrothed him to the daughter of Maharajah Krishna, Kumari Akkadevi. Virbhan was almost ecstatic when the Maharajah had accepted the proposal since his daughter was proclaimed as a genius prodigy in most of prestigious schools she had attended and other than being a girl had all the attributes of a most successful ruler.

Such were the affairs that kept Virbhan occupied but also didn't do anything to satisfy that ambitious streak in him. Overtime, Virbhan started thinking of which other kingdom he could claim and become an emperor – a Maharaja. Doing this was not simple - given that a war, no matter how justified it was, would cause a big stir in the booming economy and no one knew what turn of events could unfold as a war of that magnitude unfolded. He had asked some of his councilors about this and they had suggested offering some smaller Thakurs to pay monthly tributaries. Although he understood that this would help make the kingdom even more prosperous, this wasn't really what he had in mind. Virbhan knew that no matter how hard he tried, all the tributaries would be nullified at his death. Given that he was already above the average life expectancy of around thirty-five he wanted to do something more permanent - *for his dynasty, for his son.* Virbhan decided that he is going to have at least one more war – one that would crown him an emperor. He is going to attack the kingdom of Karakota to the West – and he is going to do that when the enemy is at their weakest – When Karakota, in turn, is at war with its own western neighbor, The Kingdom of Zunbil. This should not only make it easier for him to take over the lightly defended eastern regions of the Karakota kingdom but since majority of its forces would be in west, fighting Zunbil, it would result in a less than optimal situation for the Kingdom of Karakota to strike back. □

He sent his chancellor to start fabricating claims on various counties in Karakota. He asked his mother, the spymaster to focus on spreading lies as well as general disorder. This would help irritate the general public and administration of the ruler and make the work of fabricating claims a much easier. The results were quite encouraging. Soon Virbhan had claims for Lahur and Trigartha and was looking forward to more. From the way things were going, it should not be too difficult a task.

One day a messenger brought news of sudden losses experienced by the Karakota in its war at the western front. This was good news indeed. The king decided to make his move and he asked his marshal, Jayashakti, to start amassing his armies on the western borders of his kingdom. In about half a month Jayashakti reported that his army are as ready as they will ever be. Virbhan knew the time to strike was now when the iron was hot. With claims on six out of nine counties in Karakota he gave the order to press those claims. Virbhan had also hired a company of five hundred mercenaries that when added to his army of thousand soldiers should easily be able tilt the odds in his favor against an army of eleven hundred soldiers from Karakota –

*especially when they would be tired and wounded from an already ongoing war with the Zunbil empire.*

In the next ten days, Virbhan's armies claimed victory after victory and claimed three mid-sized counties. He received a missive from Jayashakti congratulating him of the victories but also expressing something that his marshal couldn't really figure out. Jayashakti was expecting to meet a stronger resistance at the forts they had captured, however they turned out to be an almost skeleton staff and hence none of the sieges last longer than a few days. Virbhan wondered how and why that would be the case. How could Maharaja Jaiyapada of the Karakota empire be that naïve to leave his eastern flank open like that in middle of a war. *Surely, he couldn't have been weakened that much!*

On a different front Virbhan had received news of Kumari Akkadevi starting from her capital to visit his palace on an invitation from the royal mother. It is an occasion for great celebration and is considered highly auspicious for the royal mother to bless the to-be prince's wife. Virbhan was hoping to win this war by the time Akkadevi comes to the palace and declare to everyone how Akkadevi is a blessing from the gods for the Tomara kingdom. □

One night, Virbhan woke up startled by the high-pitched cries of soldiers. He was informed that there has been a murder in the castle and the soldiers are trying to find the assassin. The one murdered was the servant of his daughter and was gifted to her by her fiancée prince. *Who would try to murder her servant? And why?* He realized that his mother, the spymaster, has been away from the palace too long and hence no one has been monitoring any plots for a long time. Looking at how successfully the war was going, and the amount of unrest in the Karakota kingdom, he estimated that his chancellor should be able to acquire the last two claims without any further need of his spymaster. He asked for dispatches to be sent to inform the spymaster to immediately start for the capital. However, he knew regardless, it would take at least three to four days given how far is the county where his mother is right now.

The search for assassin continued throughout the night without any results. The next morning the king went to see the site of the murder. When he entered the room, he was shocked to see the site. On the wall, was written in blood, "MARRIAGE WILL CAUSE TOTAL DESTRUCTION". Virbhan was angry to his core but thought of his daughter who he knew would surely have been told about this message. He went to meet her and spent the rest of the day assuring her that he would not let any harm come to her or her fiancée. He sent an urgent missive to her fiancée informing him and his father of this incident and asked to let him know of any piece of information that might help find the assassin. All this commotion from the last night and today had completely exhausted Virbhan. He thought of his son and if he can ask him to oversee the investigation and taking care of his sister while he can get some shut eye. He sent out a guard to find and fetch his prince.

While he waited for the prince to be back, he watched the strategic map of the war field in front of him and realized that he should be getting a war report any time soon. *I am surely getting too old for all this!* he thought. A call from a servant bowed in front of him woke him up. "We are unable to find the prince anywhere sire. He seems to not be anywhere in the palace.", reported the servant. Virbhan felt a chill in his chest and his arms. *Has the assassin... my son...* Virbhan was outraged. He ordered his sharpest soldiers to go and look for the prince outside the palace in his usual hangout spots. As they were heading out, they spotted the prince coming back on his horse and told him that the king is urgently looking for him. "Father, I had just gone out for a walk after such a tumultuous night. I would surely have let you know if I knew it would cause you such difficulty!", said Rajputra. It was close to night already and Rajputra asked the king to be allowed to help oversee the night watch so that the king can get some rest to which Virbhan agreed without any questions. □

As the sun was setting and the lamps were being lit, a messenger fully wrapped in thick cotton cloth was observed riding towards the palace. The messenger stopped a long way away before the palace gate, dismounted and unwrapped himself of the cloth, put the cloth on the horse and set the horse running back to where it came from. It was all very strange for the palace guards who watched all this from afar. The messenger took a few steps but fell down on the ground. When the guards approached him, they found him dead due to exhaustion, over-sweating, and overheating, possibly due to being wrapped in that thick cloth and riding during daytime. There was a note that slipped out of his hands that had the king's seal and it was delivered to the king as soon as possible. What it said, made Virbhan freeze where he was standing.

IT'S THE BLACK PLAGUE, CLOSE THE GATES, KILL AND BURN ANYONE WHO BRINGS YOU THIS MESSAGE! Our army will die. Karakota's armies will die. I will hold the army here as much as possible before they all find out what's wrong, decide to revolt and run back to their home.

Your faithful servant

Jayashakti

For the first time in his life, Virbhan did not know how to respond. He stood in silence as he looked at the guard looking at him for his order. Virbhan realized the person looking at him needs to be contained. "Everyone except you. Leave us.", he said to the guard and everyone in the room. "You two at the door come in", he said, realizing the guards at the door would be the ones who were the closest to him as he came in. "Wait here", he said, as the three people stood in front of him bowed down and he walked out of the room. He disrobed and threw his clothes outside the room. Without even asking him two servants started picking up the clothes and gear on the ground. He grimaced and told them to go back inside the room and wait with the guards until further orders. Virbhan felt his heartbeat with every step he took. On reaching the other side of the corridor he called for his commander and asked the servants to bring him another set of clothes. He also commanded that everyone needs to avoid the throne room at all costs. *It's the most valuable room in the palace. I cannot destroy that room!!! But then for how long will you keep people out of that room??? For as long as it takes!!!* The commander appeared and was shocked to see the king without any clothes. Intuitively, he at once went into a defensive position. Virbhan whispered to him in the calmest voice he could muster at the moment, "We have the plague. Do not enter the throne room. There are five people in it. Call them out. Make them walk outside somewhere in an open area. Kill them there. Make sure they do not touch or drop anything on their way there. Do not tell them anything otherwise they might try to run and touch others. The throne room stays locked until we are rid of the plague. Close the palace gates. Make it look like the normal evening place gate closure. The gates do not open until I say so." Virbhan could hear the commander's armor chink as his posture shifted from defensive to one of a panic. The commander bowed in one of the slowest bows Virbhan had seen him make. It was like his body was refusing to move. To kill the very people who report to him and follow his order blindly, without even telling them what was wrong - It chilled him to the bone. However, he knew this had to be done. ☐

Virbhan moved slowly and at once everything else felt meaningless and easy to cope with than this invisible enemy that had shown up on his gate. He knew that he should sleep that night, but sleep escaped him. He had butterflies in his stomach. He tried to imagine how will everyone react tomorrow morning when the gates would not open. He tried to imagine that his soldiers had given those five people a quick death, but the fact they couldn't get close to them made him think otherwise. He thought of his armies and if this war was worth it. He thought of his faithful marshal Jayashakti. He then thought of the revolting army. He thought of his own army trying to break the door to his palace. He heard the loud THUD of the bartering ram on the palace door. As he woke up startled, he saw the door to his room open and, his steward, Kamal, enter and bow in front of him. "Sire, commander Chakrayudha tells me that the doors to the palace and the throne room have been closed on your orders. This has concerned most of the courtiers and all are waiting for you to address any situation we should know about. Kindly let us know where and when would you like us to be present." Virbhan realized he had surrounded himself with paintings of his family before he fell sleep on his table. As he looked at those a shiver ran down his spine – his wife and mother were still outside and on way to the palace. *Are they infected? What should I do with them? How do I let them in? Should I let them in? WE NEED TO FIND A CURE!!!!* His eyes fell on his daughters' image. *At least they are safe and thank God we had the prince overseeing the security. WE NEED TO FIND A CURE!!!* "Call the royal physician at once", he yelled. The guards ran. Virbhan realized that although Kamal is finding it hard to believe his own suspicions and his trying to disregard the obvious panic evident on his king's but all this is definitely making him think something not too far from reality. Virbhan needed to ensure that the palace is not panicking once they hear this news. "Kamal, please ask everyone to meet me in the gardens."

As the news spread, everyone reacted to it in different ways. Some stayed calm, some pretended to stay calm and then some other panicked – those few who couldn't be controlled were jailed by a court consensus. The royal physician was asked to start working on a cure – however everyone knew this was a lost cause – there was no cure against the black plague. Those who were calm were still scared of the army revolting and coming back. Everyone expressed concerns but offered no solutions to the queen and the king mother coming back. □

It had been about five days when the royal cook appeared before Virbhan and told him that since the palace doors are closed, there is no new food supplies entering the palace. The upcoming food shortage needed to be planned for and the royal cook provided a couple of options ranging from rationing to fasting. Initially fasting was chosen but it was found that people would eat more on the day following the fast and hence the second option was applied hastily. Although everyone welcomed this option initially but soon almost everyone became disgruntled with the lack of food and almost always being hungry. There were a couple of arrests of servants who were trying to steal food. Courtiers argued that it was their masters who had asked the poor servants to steal food and keeping these servants in jail is injustice against poor. *How quickly the silk curtains of decorum come down when people are hungry and disgruntled*, thought Virbhan, when a messenger from his palace guard handed him a message.

The queen and the royal mother have been spotted in the town outside the palace. From what we can observe from inside the castle, it looks like they are trying to assuage people to stay calm. They also look like they are in good health. However, if we let them inside, there is a chance that we might also let in some other infected peasants. If, however, your majesty commands we can plan a mission which would be done in complete secrecy and would retrieve the queen and the royal mother through the secret tunnels under the palace. If, however, such a mission is to be carried out I recommend we only bring back the queen and the royal mother to ensure no one else learns of the existence of the secret tunnels. Moreover, I would highly recommend ensuring no one else learns that the queen and royal mother have been brought in the palace, since that might cause other court officials to start asking to bring their family members inside the palace complex.

Your humble servant

Chakrayudha

Virbhan was torn, scared, anxious, desperate, chilled, outraged - all at the same time. He knew he wanted to say yes. He knew that he would not say yes if it was anyone else. He knew that his queen and his mother would not expect him to say yes. He knew that he loved his family too much to not say yes. It had to be done. But if they are infected, the disease could spread to his children as well. *To him as well! I don't care for myself... but my children... I can't do that to them! Really, do you not care for yourself??? Really? Who are you lying to? We cannot wait forever before deciding. This has to be done before the court learns of their presence outside.* The king goes to his physician, Guru Ramkalpa, and finds he has lost most of his body weight and is a walking skeleton. With tears in his eyes, Virbhan manages to contain his emotions for his old guru and asks him if he has found a cure, but the physician has no good news for him. Virbhan asks if the physician has found a way to find if someone is infected or not, to which Ramkalpa replies that he has indeed found a method to find if someone is infected or not. He had not reported that to the since he has been focused on finding a cure. "O gurudev, this is great news indeed! One that we needed badly. I will not stop you from what you are doing. However, kindly keep me informed of even the smallest progress you make." Says Virbhan to his guru and leaves the room with the hope that he won't have to keep his queen and mother in isolation if they are not infected - *which of course they are not!!! How can they be??? They have so many servants that ensure they stay safe. Of course, they are safe, and we can find that out! God is on my side! God is on my side!* □

Virbhan gives the orders. In the deep void of night, a company of king's most trusted guards and the captain move out to retrieve the queen and royal mother. The company has orders to kill anyone who might report this rescue – which includes most of the queen and royal mother's maidens and guards who are on duty and awake that night. Kill after kill the company nears the queen and royal mother's chambers where they hear an argument going on with a familiar third voice. It's the prince!!! *What the hell is he doing here??? How the hell did he get out??? Did he ... secret tunnels??? Sigh.*

The captain enters the chamber and finds another girl in the corner who he has never seen before. He bows and lets the room know of his mission and all are to follow him in absolute silence. At this point everyone agrees, and the prince takes the girl's hand in his hand to which the queen and mother interrupt him, "She is not going in whether you like it or not. We can all stay here or we three can go in. Kumari Akkadevi is on her way to the capital, and we cannot have you floundering around with this street dancer from nowhere. It is not only unbecoming of you as a prince but also puts your upcoming marriage in danger. Think about it!!!" The prince is visibly becoming angry as he is listening to his mother and grandmother. As the captain watched the argument unfold, he realizes what is happening. *Has he gone nuts!!! Is thinking of marring this girl???!!! How can he not know this is impossible???!!!* "Your high-ness, can we sort this out once we are in the palace. We can surely come and get anyone we are ordered to rescue once you, the queen and royal mother are inside the palace. Please consider this servant's request as most urgent at this hour.", Chakrayudha beseeched the prince. "Captain, this is a family matter. I suggest you do not interfere. Mother, Royal Mother, I cannot leave Radha here since she can become infected if she stays here. Me and her are one, both in this life and in the next. I cannot live in this world without seeing her beautiful face in front of me as I start my day. It is true love that I bring to you. One that is beyond rank or riches, beyond walls and halls. Please mothers, take us in for if you cannot take both of us in, then I cannot go with you as well. I will have to take a different route and ask our king of justice on the palace door just like all the rest.", said the prince and starts heading out of the chamber at which point, the queen understands the seriousness of the situation and agrees to take the girl with them.

The company heads out and quietly reaches to a remote area around the palace walls where the entrance to secret tunnel opens up. At that moment, the queen orders Chakrayudha, "Kill her!". Seeing this a duel ensues between the prince trying to protect the girl who he asks to run away and finally runs away himself. The captain who is trying to practice restraint while fighting the prince gets injured. The queen and the royal mother to escort the captain back to the palace before he loses too much blood. They find Ramkalpa standing outside the door when they enter the palace. He decides that since the captain has also been injured by a potentially infected weapon, he would have to test the captain as well. Until he gets the results all three are asked to wait in the same room.

The results take a few hours but in the end the queen and the royal mother are declared as not infected but the captain has caught the infection due to the blood wound. The queen and the royal mother thank him and ask him if he could isolate himself in a room and he duly agrees. Virbhan thanks the company and the captain for his bravery and promises to take care of his family after him "in case Ramkalpa is not able to find a cure". "Who are you kidding sire. We both know how likely Ramkalpa is to find a cure for this before it becomes serious. It has been an honor serving my king. Please don't tell my family how I passed away." "Chakrayudha, I give you my word that all of us and your family would be proud of you." Virbhan gives his captain a final bow before walking away. He asks the queen and the royal mother to sequester themselves in an isolated part of the palace and stay there until the plague has passed. □

As Virbhan reaches back to his palace, it is getting close to morning and people are starting to gather around the gates pleading to open them. He is informed that one of the people in the gathering is the prince himself and is yelling that he would reveal the routes to the secret tunnels if he is not let in with a girl he wants to bring inside.

*What an idiot!!!! What an idiot!!! How the hell is he even outside??? Means he was not helping with the palace security oversight??? Argh... What an idiot this son of mine is. Sigh what will he do when he is king. He would be eaten alive!!! Argh...* Virbhan is not sure how to deal with this. He calls his most trusted advisors to help him out all of whom are flabbergasted when they hear of what is happening at the door. They caution the king that letting the prince in will be publicly seen as ruthless injustice and probably will cause civil riots. On the other hand, if the prince reveals the locations of the secret tunnels, it is as good as opening the gates, or even worse since these tunnels are designed with minimal security features to allow quick escape. Protecting the palace from all these tunnels would be close to impossible without exposing the soldiers to the plague itself at which point the castle soldiers who are already on a diet will most likely revolt.

After much deliberation a third option is finalized. Smiths are asked to prepare a special type of arrow. Its blunt and heavy on impact. The archers use these to strike down the prince and the girl until they are unconscious. The other people at the door are shocked at the treatment however, return home talking about how it was also just in a way. Late night when everyone has gone back the door is opened a slit and the two bodies lying down are pulled in. They are both tested by the physician and declared safe; however, they are both caged separately in the palace courtyard. At this point Virbhan feels he has no other option but to provide a display of justice to allow for his son to blackmail the palace to be let in in such a way. Virbhan feels that letting him stay outside caged for the night should give him a reality check.

As if there was no end to his troubles, he is informed very early morning of yet another murder. This time it is as he feared – it is his daughter. The words "DON'T WORRY MY JOB IS DONE" have been smeared over the walls of her room. The king loses himself. *IT IS ALL BECAUSE OF THIS *$%&#*%#*

*RASCAL!!! ALL I ASKED WAS TO LOOK OUT FOR HIS SISTER.... BUT NO... HE WAS TOO BUSY IN HIS LOVE AFFAIR!!! AND THAT GIRL!!! THEY WILL PAY!!!* He rushes out and orders the girl to be punished by Immurement – death by caging inside walls of stone. The prince is made to watch as the walls of heavy stone go up around this girl he has loved. After the wall is completed, the prince is released from his cage and ordered to stay in a small part of the palace. Virbhan goes back to his dead daughter and feels he has left nothing to live for. He has seen the worst that can happen to him and his family. Days pass slowly and Virbhan refuses to come out of mourning. All this time Rajkalpa keeps him company and feeds him potions to keep up the king's health – all the while the king can see his guru's body starting to crumble before him. To help him face this period Rajkalpa even allows the queen and the royal mother to move back to the king's quarters as long as they do not make their presence known outside.

One day a guard comes to his room running. "Your highness, the prince has runaway and is reported to have commandeered our army. He has rallied our army to attack the palace and to take your kingdom. Sire we do not have enough troops to hold back the prince".

Virbhan looks to his right to his queen and watches tears run down her eyes. He doesn't know what to think anymore. His chest is heavy, and he finds it hard to breath. Darkness comes softly. ∎

# QUEEN MOTHER

The mood in the capital of Udabhandh was full of sorrow and tears. Rajah Bahadur Singh had just passed away at an early age of forty-five. Queen Prabhadevi had asked her son, Prince Trilokyachandra to return home from his foreign education at the world-renowned university of Takshashila. She knew that this would be the end of Prince's education at the university, as the kingdom would need a king soon.

Prince Trilok, as he was more affectionately called, was renowned for being as much a genius as he was stubborn. He had explicitly refused all help from his father to get accepted at the acclaimed university since he wanted to do it on his own. Although many doubted if some favor was still used when the prince got admitted to the institution so quickly after the exam, it was made clear time and again, that it was due to the extraordinary brilliance of the prince when results started getting posted with the prince at the top of his class term after term. The Acharya – the principle for the university, had conversed with Rajah Bahadur at multiple times if he would allow the prince to even teach some classes but the king had refused each time. Bahadur was concerned that this might make his genius son into an academician instead of a leader. Now, the queen hoped her son had matured to the point where he could understand his responsibilities and how they mattered much more than his keen interest in his academic pursuits.

Endless series of rites and rituals filled the next few weeks. The prince was getting his first taste of carrying himself in the court as the soon-would-be-king. Although the queen worried that prince might be too young for all this responsibility – *He is just seventeen!* – she kept thinking. The next few weeks were to be a learning experience for both mother and son. Prabhadevi learned to her heart's content that her son is handling himself quite well and seems to be gaining everyone's respect in the court. She also wanted to get him married as soon as possible since she understood how important it had become that the kingdom has an heir.

It was about a month from the day of Prince's coronation when Prabhadevi was informed of the prince's unusual decision. Prince Trilokyachandra had decided to split his marriage into two parts – the first part had to do strictly with the marriage formalities and the second to do with the month-long celebrations. Prince had decided to complete the first step in the next five days, and he had asked the Royal Pundit to complete all formalities in a single day! This had never been done before. This confused queen, as she had not even spoken to Prince Trilok about the different potential brides. She wanted to understand who he would want to get married to, but it seemed like all decisions had already been taken.

The queen went to her son's quarters and found him in discussions with some senior court ministers and the court guru. *This late!!! I hope everything is ok.* "May we have a moment alone?" she politely asked the ministers who bowed and started walking backwards. "Honorable ministers and guru" said the prince and the ministers halted their retreat. "Mother, are you here to ask me about my decision to split my marriage into two parts? If that is the case, I request you to allow my elders, our ministers and court guru to stay and partake this conversation" Prabhadevi was not only without any options but was quite surprised by the request. *Why does he want them to stay ???! what does it have to do with them??? By the looks of it, it seems they already know something I don't. Oh child, you are too young to know this game of politics. I hope you are not too generous in your trust and know that these people won't trust you that quickly. You will have to earn their respect. I hope you know what you are doing!!!* It seemed that the prince could judge what his mother was thinking. "Mother, please do not worry. I don't want to do anything that causes any harm to the family, however, there are some things that need to be completed before we can truly settle down to have a month of festivity. I understand that coronation cannot wait and so does the marriage." Prabhadevi looked at his son with a quizzical look. "That said, I am quite certain that father did not trouble you with the details our armies marching north towards Pamir." "No, he didn't. But what does that have to do with your marriage?" For a moment, the prince seemed to be thinking how to explain the details most clearly to his mother. "The winters this year – they are going to be much worse than the last five years combined. You know this already mother. Everyone knows how busy you have been to ensure that the capital has enough supplies of food, cloth, and medicine for the coming winter. Father trusted you to do this as much as himself so that he could focus on what is going outside the capital and around the kingdom." *I see now. He is trying to arrange for supplies for our armies outside the capital. But why meddle with his marriage to do that.* She kept listening. "As you might have already guessed, we have armies on march and encamped in allied territories that were depending on father to arrange supplies for them this winter. We are not in a direct war with anyone, instead, we are in an allied war and are trying to support some of our partners. These partners have been able to focus on trade and commerce while they have had a stronger ally such as us. I am really sorry to bother you with all the details, but all this would not have needed me to change my marriage plans if it was not some kings who decided that they could take advantage of father's absence to attack and finish off our armies. Some of those enemies have shifted their focus from our allies to us instead. Once I get married, I would request you to help the bride settle down in the palace while I take care of this business. It should only take a month or so and after that we can have a good time as a family." The ministers looked at her and quietly nodded. *Has he already convinced them???! You idiots, why are you listening to this kid!??? Well... they are not idiots. Bahadur trusted them... they know what they are doing... Or have they convinced him of this!??? No... no... that cannot be... they wouldn't do that... Argh... curse our enemies. O' my lovely child, why did such a burden fall on you so soon!!!* "As to who I will marry is also something I have decided. Please allow me to be as bold as to suggest if I can marry the Rajkumari (Princess) Vijyavati." Prabhadevi's eyes bulged out of their sockets. *What is he talking about!!!??? Has he even seen her???!!! So many have told me how ugly she is. This boy will surely make us the laughingstock of the world. All those things she keeps tinkering with has caused so many stains on her skin and face. Why her??? Why her my son???* "Why her Trilok? I have selected so many others for you that you haven't even looked at even once." The prince seemed to know what his mother was thinking. "Mother, please allow me to marry Vijyavati. She is brilliant and a renowned chemist. She is quite learned and very respected in many academic fields where only men are allowed to partake." *This boy has gone mad... is he selecting a wife or a court physician...!!! Does he know he doesn't need his wife to read scriptures to him???!!! I wish his father were here right now.* The prince continued, "Mother, she comes from a great house and that would help us in case we need support in our conquest in Pamir" this seemed to anchor something in the queen. "How do we know they will come to our aid? Son, you are assuming too much for too little." "Mother, you already know that Rajkumari Vijyavati is lacking the good looks that princes look for." *YES, I DO, AND YOU SHOULD AS WELL!!!!* "It is for this reason her father is extremely grateful to us for me marrying his only daughter whose hand no one else is accepting. Mother, at the very least please consider it a blessing you grant on your kingdom as a queen but also something you would allow your son to decide for himself, the person, he would like to spend his whole life with. Right after marriage I would go through a coronation ceremony, which again, I have asked the guru to perform with the most important rites and customs - so that it can be finished in a few hours. I expect the only audience to be the court members and some of our important allies who could afford to get here by that time." By this time, it was clear how flustered Prabhadevi was. "Mother, do not be concerned. I don't wish to do away with all the festivities and celebrations – I merely want to delay them to the point when we have secured our position. Once back, we shall have the royal coronation and wedding in their full glory along with the fact that your son has already proven himself in battle." The prince knew he couldn't say anything more that could convince her queen. *Mother...I know it's hard to accept what I am saying... However, if not me, please trust the advisors you and father have had for so many years.*

Prabhadevi stood speechless at the edge of a decision; only her darting eyes belying her stillness. She could not say no. She was getting her wish – to get her son married. The queen could also not turn away from her duties to the kingdom. Something in her lifted her hand and put it on her son's shoulders. "Go. Follow your elders." She turned towards the ministers and the guru – assumed a position of command as their queen. Her head held high, breathing heavy and her teary eyes issuing commands as she looked at them. *"They have been with your father as they will be with you, and they WILL ensure their king's safe return."* Everyone bowed in front of their queen as she turned around with a heavy heart. *My son, oh my lovely child... be safe...* □

On the day of marriage, the prince was quite surprised how much truth the rumors held about the rajkumari's looks. She looked nothing like a princess. More like a boy peasant with feminine features - one who would have skin with rough patches and boils as a result of months of working at the local tannery. Throughout the ceremonial rites the prince could hear giggles and whispers in the crowd that he could only guess were pointed at his would-be bride and very possibly his intelligence for such a decision. He kept focusing on what should he say to Vijyavati in the evening when they would get a few hours together before he leaves for battle tomorrow.

Evening came and he walked towards the prince's chamber that was smelling of luscious perfume while the palace halls reverberated with the sound of melodious music specially created for this occasion. As he moved closer to the door, Trilok tried to imagine various things he could talk to his new wife about – he however, somewhat knowing about the princess's personality, was concerned about how he should approach her in the first place. Should he completely feign ignorance for how ugly she is and tell her that he thinks she is beautiful to him; or should he be bold and let her know that he understands how she looks but he doesn't care. *How would she react if I do that??? Oh my, how would anyone react to that... that is so disrespectful. Sigh.* After many moments the prince realized he was standing still - on the edge of the door. *I am sure by all this noise the princess knows I am standing here and thinking all these things... argh... how stupid of me... I shouldn't look too fast or careless or callous, but I shouldn't look too sentimental as well. I should enter at a medium pace.* With calculated precision, the prince carefully increased the weight behind his hand as he pushed the door forward and stepped in. He looked towards the bed where the princess would be – all dressed up for the prince to take his first close look at his bride. The bed, however, was empty. The prince looked around and found the door to the balcony opened and he walked towards that with a curious feeling; a smile appeared on his face. *Games???!!!???*

"Prince Trilokyachandra!", the prince's feet stopped in middle of a step with that sound from somewhere at the back of the room. "Tell me why you chose me as your wife." The prince gritted his teeth as he turned thinking of how to answer this question. He tried to utter something polite and meaningful but couldn't form a sentence after the initial "I..." The next few moments the prince stood at the same spot making sounds telling of his inability to articulate anything meaningful, pretending to be thinking of a decent answer and mostly breathing or making sounds such as "aaaa..." or "ummm..."

"May I take a stab at it?" said the princess. *Huh!* "Umm... please" the prince looked at the princess's figure facing the wall wondering what he is going to hear forgetting to close his mouth. "Your highness, we both know you did not marry me for my exceptional beauty." The prince almost broke in a giggle and clenched his teeth and lips to look serious. "I also know about your... our ??? armies in the north. With you having just started your reign it makes sense to have support from a powerful ally such as my father to gain legitimacy as a strong ruler quickly." *She has done her research quite...* "I am sure you don't mind my father's armies providing the extra support as well... Am I correct so far?" *...well. I am not sure where she is going to take this. I need to turn this around...* "Umm... well, all this you said, does help, but that is not the only reason… I know about your renown in the field of medicine, strategy…” “Are you telling me you've married me because I am a good physician ???” *gulp…* “Well not exactly…” *I need to think about this…* the prince took a deep breath and stood there for many moments. The princess waited silently. The prince thought of something that although made sense to him but wasn't sure if he knew how to word properly or if his wife would understand or even agree with. As moments passed, silence became deafening. At some point his lips started forming words, and he realized that he was stammering. His only hope was to speak what he was thinking.

“As a princess you know, as royalty, we do not have the same freedom as a farmer working in the fields. Well, we could of course do whatever we want to but that won't work very well for the kingdom now, would it? In my wife, I did not intend to see a beautiful girl. I intend to meet my friend, my best friend, who is able to understand my pains and help me solve my problems – the problems of our country.” Something took hold of the prince. Like some ancient knowledge he had received from his gurus in Takshashila, at once, he could see a bigger picture... in a moment, his mind and heart were one... there was a bigger meaning in front of him... he spoke about the clarity in his mind... more to teach himself what he was seeing than anyone else. "Not only what you said about your father supporting me and our armies, is completely true, but my view of what my wife is also something you completely embody. Your candor tells me you are quite comfortable with how you look and are not one to hide behind walls because of that. In fact, you have the boldness I have looked for everywhere and I consider myself lucky to be able to get such an ability in my wife. If I would have married you for your academic abilities it would have been foolish of me, however, I am not one to discard the genius so rarely found in women of royal birth and upbringing. On the contrary, all the spoiled brats I've had the unfortunate chance to meet has helped strengthen my resolve of what is more important and what is not." Silence. "Are you not concerned how ugly our children would be?" The prince's voice was calm like a buddha. "As long as they know how to successfully manage the country, they can be as ugly as they could be, and I would still be proud of them." Something jingled. The prince almost woke up from a dream to see the princess turning and walking towards him. He saw the smiling face of a trusting friend looking at him. "Are you hungry? I am hungry. Let's eat something.", she said and called for the servants. □

The next few years passed quickly. The prince, now the king, had been able to assert his superiority over his foes and in turn able to resume trade with old trade partners. Prabhadevi, now the queen mother, had grown used to her daughter-in-law. Later she fell sick and barely made it alive, the royal physician let her know that he had almost given up, but it was the queen's knowledge of medicine that had helped him to save her. The fact that Vijyavati never even let her know of how much she worked for her health hit her deep in heart. Since that day both the queen and the queen mother became a single team, taking care of the palace, the court and capital in whatever way they could. The king had a boy, Gautamdeva, and a girl, Gauridevi, who by chance, took their features from their father. Although he was congratulated by courtiers here and there for that, the king never made a big deal of it. Instead, Vijyavati teased him of having an affair with someone else "otherwise the kids should have looked like her". He was proud of her, and she knew that.

As time passed some of the old advisors passed away and court positions opened up. Trilokyachandra was surprised when one day his marshal, Yudhakalpa, and senior minister, Sitender Singh, came to him suggested if he would consider Vijyavati as his chief spymaster. "Your highness, the queen is quite literally managing all of that already. Our late last spymaster Jagannath always worked with the queen and us to ensure the security of the palace as well as our contacts overseas. We are quite lucky to have a queen as herself who already knows this role and quite obviously, your highness would not find anyone as trustworthy as the queen herself." A chill dawned on the king. He knew what the role entailed. The last spymaster had spent many years in the northern kingdoms spying and stealing secrets. *I can't have Vijyavati do that. I cannot live without her.... What about the children...* the minister saw emotions fly on the king's face and understood what he was thinking. "Maybe we should leave for now and give your highness some time to think about it."

The king adjourned the court for the day and found himself unable to think of anything. His mind was frozen. *I cannot lose my love... my friend... who else is here...* Every name he came up with didn't seem to have the skills to match the role. He knew someone needed to be recruited soon but he also knew at this time, the court wouldn't approve of someone from outside. The mysterious circumstances in which Jagannath had died meant that someone had learned of his identity and might be trying to plant a spymaster in his court. The king wandered aimlessly in the palace until a servant informed him that the queen is asking for him at the dinner table.

As he entered the dining room, he found a person he was not expecting there. It was his cousin sister, Tulsidevi, a widow and at his court since last many years. *Why is she here…???* Vijyavati had asked her to settle in the palace to "help her deal with the trauma" and nanny the kids when she was busy with court affairs. Trilok greeted his sister and sat down and gave the queen a puzzled look. Food was served and they started eating with small talk around the table. "You must have heard about Jagannath" said the queen abruptly. The king could hear almost his heartbeat. He knew they both had always put the country in front of their own since the day they met. He did not like where this could go. "You know Tulsi has been taking care of the kids since the last many years." The queen's eyes met the king's eyes. She could see how heavily the king was breathing. She got up, stood behind him, bent and put her arms around him. "You know I will still be there, my love. You know it needs to be me..." The king didn't like where this was going. He tried to wiggle his way out of the queen's embrace. "...for now. At least until we find someone suitable. It's not going to be long love." The king knew she was right. *no... no... no...* His eyes were closed tight and kept shaking his head. A warm cheek pressed next to his and whispered "...I promise my love." A soft palm slowly rubbed off his moist eyes, "Open your eyes my highness. This is not the time to think about your personal happiness. Think about your duty to the kingdom and if you can afford to stop the work Jagannath was doing to go in vain. If we don't find who is extorting the traders coming into our boundaries, think about how much it can impact our relations with the Chinese emperor. Can we afford that your highness?" The king knew what she was saying was right. *but I could send my army and... sigh... that would alert them... a reward ??? yea, we know how well they work... we'll just get a thousand fake reports while the bandits keep doing their thing...argh... wait a minute... let me ask her only... if she is that smart... let her figure it out...* the king opened his eyes and saw Tulsi and kids looking at him silently. "My love" he whispered, "why don't you think of another plan. I am sure you can do it!" the queen walked away at once and stood at the other end of the room looking out of the window. "Do you think it is easy for me?" the king could hear the solitary cricket outside in the garden. Vijyavati's voice was crisp and cold now. "Your highness, as royalty, we do not have the same freedom as a farmer working in the fields. Well, we could of course do whatever we want to but that won't work very well for the kingdom now, would it?" Hearing the same statement after so many years, the king's heart sank. "Tulsi, kindly take the kids away." And then she added, "Take care of them like your own" Tulsi bowed and retired herself with the children. The king saw a mother fake a sad smile as the kids looked at her in puzzlement as Tulsidevi walked them out of the room. □

The next day, court is told that the queen is departing on a long-term tour of the country and is helping the poor of the nation in whatever way she can. People are suspicious, but when they see and hear of the queen in various parts of the country, they believe the story to be true. Some courtiers also approach the king and express their sympathies for the king to be without a wife and offer to gift him different concubines. However, Trilokyachandra refuses all those offers. The king hears whispers about these same people being quick to dismiss any mention of the queen's pain. They generally dismiss it saying, "how ugly she is", which in their minds was same as she wouldn't find anyone to love or have need of love anyways. The king is enraged but the queen tells him to keep his wits about him since the court ignoring her absence in general is only helping his cause.

A few months afterwards a messenger hands the king a sealed message that speaks of the bandit case finally being solved and those responsible being handled by the marshal and senior ministers. Inside the message, he also finds recommendations on how to present this victory to the Chinese Emperor Huang. *Finally... she can come back home.* The king breathes a sigh of relief and sends his messengers to both Emperor Huang as well as to Vijyavati. The emperor treats this news as a big victory since it is the same group of bandits that were terrorizing other parts of the silk road. The king finds it quite discomforting when, his marshal, stops him short of completing his sentence in the court where he wanted to announce celebrations to welcome the return of Vijyavati. *He knows something that I don't.* "Your highness, please allow me to discuss queen's travel plans with you and perhaps we can plan anything after that. Since it involves the security of the queen I could only do it in private with your highness." The king earmarks this discussion in a few days from then however, he receives another message from Vijyavati the very next day.


My love,

I know you want me back in the court. However, I can accomplish much more for our kingdom where I am than in the capital. The bandits that we have been able to crush had been supported by the kings of Skardu, Leh and Kangra. They want to divert the silk road towards their kingdoms, but little do they know that the silk road is where it is not only because of political power and infrastructure but also due to difficulty of crossing natural terrain elsewhere. Their ego and inability to understand these basic concepts have helped me not only quicken my efforts in fabricating claims to their kingdom but also motivate some strong families to voice out their concerns against them. Kindly consider using the claims to these kingdoms I am sending to you along with this message to end this problem once for all. If not done, these kingdoms will only grow more confidant overtime and will do everything to loosen our grip on the trade routes. I understand that attacking three kingdoms in a single stroke seems ambitious, however, I am expecting you to hear from those families very soon that I hope would help you make up your mind for this conquest.

My love, please do not worry about me. I am quite comfortable where I am. Sitender Singh and Yudhakalpa are constantly at my disposal and help me with various affairs. I know you will find a way to discreetly recognize them for their efforts throughout my time away from you.

Although I miss being with the one man I love so much, helping my liege in managing his kingdom gives me immense happiness and pride. Please convey my gratitude to Tulsi and give my love to our children.

Eternally yours

Vijyavati

*Sigh...* He looks behind the message and sees attached various other documents and spots the claims to the kingdoms amongst those. He looks at Yudhakalpa and Sitender Singh in the eye with sadness. *You knew about all this... It's not your wife who is not with you... how long do you think this can go on...???* They both seem to understand what their king is thinking and bow with clear signs of concern visible on their faces. "Your highness, your concerns are our concerns. However, the queen is quite resolved in purpose, and we do not dare to question her. We understand, we are guilty of bringing sadness to our highness and should be punished accordingly." And both of them drop to their knees. *Argh... why is everyone making me feel that wanting,*

*the one woman I love, with me, is so selfish!!!???
Why...??? I love her!!! She is my wife...the mother of
my children!!! Vijyavati... sigh... why did you have to
be so good at logic... and duty... and other things...
why couldn't you be more like other women...* The
king rests his forehead in his palms and stays there
for the longest time. The caw of a crow somewhere
outside snaps the king out of his reverie. Sitender
Sing and Yudhakalpa were still on their knees and
the court waiting for his orders. *Sigh... let's get this
over with...* "Rise, both of you. You both know why I
am sad, but the actions of both of you to take care
of the queen are worth recognition. Both of you shall
be rewarded with five hundred gold coins from the
royal treasury." There was quite a murmur in the
court. "Your highness is too kind! We were just
doing our duty." said Sitender Sing. Both bowed and
started walking back. "And Yudhakalpa...", the king
held out the claims to hand them to Sitender Singh.
"...prepare for war!" □

The next day, a couple of courtiers come forward with requests to introduce some of their relations in Leh and Kangra. "Sire, our lives are constantly made miserable by impractical requests by our liege to setup more infrastructure in places where we know our business will not flourish. We understand and respect the nature and the reason behind the trade route and know that setting up an alternate path is a futile exercise that will only result in us throwing our hard-earned income to no end. Please help ease our pain sire, and we shall do whatever meager help we can to help your highness with any plans he might have in the near future." Said the representative of the group and looked at the courtier who had introduced him who in turn looked the king. *Vijyavati... oh my dear spymaster... what plots are you cooking on my behalf...* The king smiled and nodded. "Sitender Singh, kindly work with these gentlemen to see how they can help with our plans in the near future."

Victory came easy as most of the enemy kingdoms were in disarray already for some reason. The king knows the queen has already been at work here spreading unrest in these areas.

It takes a few years for the newly conquered kingdoms to stabilize. However, with time, the same wealthy families that had come to the king before start threatening him of a revolt if they are not given exclusive contracts to trade on the silk road. At the same time, a rumor going around also has that there is an assassin inside the palace to get rid of the king and has been placed by the same merchants. A few days afterwards, one morning, a guard comes and lets the king know that the queen's troupe has been sighted approaching the palace. The king is overjoyed. "The court is dismissed for today!" He rides out to the troupe to welcome his queen to the palace after so many years. He almost breaks into tears seeing how much she has aged and how weak she is looking. "I am not going to let you go away now." The queen smiles silently and rests her head in the king's lap.

Trilok tries to make as much time for his wife in the next few days but mostly finds Vijyavati not in her quarters whenever he goes to meet her. On the second night he asks her about her absence when they are together. "My love, I know you have heard about the assassin in the palace" The king shakes his head to dismiss it, "That is just a rumor people..." The queen puts a figure on his lips and whispers. "It's not. In the next few days, I will be working with some of our palace engineers to ensure that we have the mechanisms in place to catch this killer in his tracks." The king now gets why she is here. She does not trust anyone else to do this. *...but what after that... she is not...* "You are not leaving after this ... please say no... you can't" "My love" the queen whispers, "I have to" *why? Why??? WHY???!!! What is so important now...???!!!* The queen sat upright and slightly distanced herself, "I know you don't like it, but let me explain" *I don't want any explanations!* The king looked away. "Do you not want to be with me? Do you want to stay like this forever? Do you not see how much I need you?" his eyes met hers. "I see that. Every day I feel the same my love. But I have gotten to a point now that I cannot stay in the capital even if I wanted to." *What is she talking about.* Confusion was evident on the king's face. The queen takes a deep breath and tries to find a way to break it to the king. She tries to put it in the softest way she could... "My love..." The king cannot wait anymore, "What is it??? What have you gotten yourself into dear??? Why can't we be together???" another deep breath... "I am working in the court of the Chinese Emperor..." A lightning bolt strikes at the very heart of the king. He could feel his face turn cold to touch and losing track of his arms and legs. He hears his heartbeat in his ears as he looks at the woman, he loves the most. "It's taken me all these years ... my highness... but now I have secured the position of the royal midwife and physician for the Emperor Huang and his first wife. With me at the emperor's court I would be able to help our kingdom in many more ways than before. We both know..." Tears rolls down the king's eyes. "My dear wife, my friend, my love..." he finds it hard to keep his head straight. The queen gently lifts his chin with her hands. The king is barely able to speak. He somehow manages to whisper, "I cannot win an argument with you. But do you really think you need to throw your life away for the kingdom? Do we not have enough? Have you... have you thought how will I live the rest of my life without you?" Trilokyachandra does not know what to say. *Why did she have to be like this... it's all my fault... I gave her too much freedom... I... I can still revert all this... I can force her to stay... I am the king...* The queen brings her eyes in front of him. *Don't even think about it...don't be stupid...* "If the emperor finds out who I am and that I was working as a spy in his court, you already know how disastrous it would be for our kingdom." She smiles and gently wipes his tears. "What we have made here is not easy. My love... we are partners. I am your queen, and I will do my part in making our kingdom as strong as I can." More tears roll down king's eyes. "Do not think of me being away. Think of both of us on a single mission. Each a wheel of the cart of our kingdom. Your successes are my successes and mine are yours. Do not think it somehow your fault that I am living this life. I feel the greatest happiness and pride when I can do my part in growing and keeping our kingdom strong. If it makes you happy, then let me say this... I would have been doing something similar even if we never got married... You know I was a physician before our marriage as well. Right?" The king nods. "Our kids are in safe hands with Tulsi. Your hands are busy with expanding and stabilizing our lands. Even if I was to stay in the palace, knowing me, do you think I would be able to be happy, just sitting here taking care of palace affairs and family matters?" The king knew the answer to that. "I know you miss me, and I miss you more than that. But that very feeling is what makes me strong to do what I do. You need to do the same. Stop looking out for me." *...what an idiotic thing to say... as if that was possible...*

"Seriously. I am not joking. I know you think it's impossible but believe me... you can do it. Also... I know you have kept yourself alone all these years as well." *...now what is she talking about...* "I have arranged a couple of my maids to personally take care of you." *...how dare she!!!...* "Don't tense up. As long as they are around you, I know you are safe. As an advantage, you can also use them to send me a message whenever you want. Would you not grant me even such a small request? Just so that I can know how my love is doing ???" *...I know exactly why you are sending these girls... I could use anyone to send a message to you... I don't need these girls for that... don't try to play smart with me !!!...* The king sat silently. "Please?" "Yea whatever..." "I am not gone forever my dear... I will be visiting... whenever I can get a leave from the court or whenever I can get a 'medical research' leave from the emperor" The king looks up and finds the smiling face of the woman he loves and who seems to be ready to give up everything she has. As his eyebrows tensed, he felt a battle of heart and mind boil up inside him. "The assassin..." she said, "don't be too surprised to find things being changed and moved around in the palace in the next few days. My leave from the emperor's court is expiring soon since I had to slow down my arrival to the capital in order to travel using the royal troupe instead of a fast horse in disguise. I would be leaving in three days and there is a lot of work to be done before that." *Are you telling me you won't have time for us even during this short stay…!!! Oh, come on!!! what is with this girl and all this damn duty…* "My love, we will have some time together. Just not as much as you wanted." *…as if you gave me an option…* "hmmm" … The queen smiled, "Now are you going to be like this all night? Please smile and let your queen know you are still in love with her as much as she thinks you are !!!" □

The palace was a flurry of activity in the next three days. The queen works with the ministers to change the layout of the lighting, security and add structural weaknesses at key points on the wooden floor to make creaking sounds if anyone is walking. The king finds out that the two girls are of Chinese origin and then it makes more sense to him why getting messages to the queen using them might be easier. The three days pass and the queen leaves the capital as quickly as she had returned. Soon the assassin is captured. When interrogated he reveals that he is from the neighboring kingdom of Nagri who quite unsurprisingly, want to weaken him to get the silk trade. Satinder Sing lets the king know that the queen has requested him to punish this assassin by converting him to a eunuch and has arranged for him to be sent to the Chinese emperor as a gift. "This would show his highness's mercy as well as let Emperor Huang know how his highness is doing everything to ensure the safety of the trade route.", says Satinder Singh as he reads the message. Quite unexpectedly, only a few days of the eunuch reaching the court of Emperor Huang, Trilokyachandra hears of the emperor attacking the kingdom Nagri and a few more. A messenger from the emperor's court has brought this news to his court as well as an offer by the emperor to rule over these kingdoms.

To dear King Trilokyachandra,

You have proven yourself time and again a true friend of the Chinese empire by defending our trade routes. Your wisdom in managing your armies across borders is exemplary and your tacticians have unsurpassed ability to conduct logistics over extreme terrain. In you I find a trusted ally of the empire as well as a dependable friend. Please accept the kingdoms of Nagri (all provinces), Hotan (all provinces) and Pangong as gift from the Chinese empire. I hope both of our houses stay strong allies in future.

Your Friend

Emperor Huang Jingzu

The whole court is taken by surprise and cheers for the king. This leads to Trilokyachandra forming the Empire of Udabhandh that spanned most of the northwestern border of India and himself gaining the prestigious title of Emperor.

Tulsi, now having the title of the "Royal Guardian" does a great job bringing up the kids as a mother would. Trilokyachandra also takes a note of how exceptionally humble the two girls are in serving him. It's also as if they know exactly what he wants and when. Although sometimes it is uncanny how they almost act exactly like Vijyavati. However. The emperor doesn't mind, as it reminds him of his love and knows it is the queen herself that is probably mentoring them on how to take care of him. He tries quite hard, but over time, he starts to almost see his queen in one of the girls but could not come to terms with marrying anyone else. He proposes to one of the girls if she would be willing to become his concubine and is surprised to find out that the girl is completely ok with his proposal. ...*All this time... was she planning on this... I am sure she was... argh... I shouldn't have fallen for it...* It was as if he had flicked a secret switch. The palace goes into a flurry of activity and before he knew he finds himself with that girl as a concubine. This time when the Trilokyachandra is visited by Vijyavati, he feels the shame and guilt of his actions and lets her know about him accepting one of her girls as a concubine. To his surprise Vijyavati almost makes light of the topic by telling him that he is not the first emperor to have concubines. When he is sacrificing so much for the country, he deserves to "live a little."

During a lunch she also asks him to send for his son to be married to the emperor's daughter soon. Moreover, she also recommends Chittajeet, the brilliant son of a close friend of hers to be interviewed for the position of spymaster. "Does this mean your work is done? Can you come back now?" The silence before the response already gave him the answer to his question. "My love, the role of a spymaster is quite demanding, and I am getting old. I just want to give some rest to my back and have finally been able to find someone who could carry this mantle for us. But my work at the emperor's court is still not done. There are many new developments in the East that we could benefit from. I am sure someone else could try to get us this information, but it would take too long and by then we would have lost our advantage with that information." He could only sigh. "Look at it like this; with me free of the responsibilities of the spymaster, I would be able to put more time in the emperor's court and possibly go out for royal expeditions with the emperor's queen and his mother more often!" At this point he felt it was useless to argue this point any further. He knew this woman in front of him has an iron will and however much she might love him, her love for her duty was much more. As he heard multiple voices in his head and found it difficult to keep a straight face. *Well then let her grind herself if that is what she wants... what am I thinking...!!! How cruel of me... Yes, keep thinking that... just finish this lunch and let her leave... you married her for her brain and that is what you got... you are foolish to look for more... shut up... just... shut up... just finish this lunch for god's sake...* "My love, I don't want to stress you even more, but can I ask you to do something for me?" He looked up with hopeless eyes. He saw the same smiling face he desired to look at all those years but never found by his side. "Just say it..." said the emperor half under his breath; too tired to say anything more. The queen waits for his eyes to meet hers. "Under no circumstance, should you allow Chittajeet to go to China; regardless of whether you make him your spymaster or not. Promise me." *...these absurd requests... she comes with those out*

*of nowhere... what am I supposed to say here...
no???!!!* "Of course..." *sigh...* "Thank you!" "eh..." □

In a few days, the queen leaves again. The emperor sends out a proposal for the prince, "Raja Gautamdeva" to be married to the emperor's daughter. The emperor accepts the proposal and in turn offers to form an alliance with the Empire of Udabhandh. The queen's absence during the prince's wedding is coordinated carefully by blaming the weather and queen's health to have her make emergency stops that prevented her from being present at the marriage ceremony. Gautamdeva, never knew his mother and for him this was one of the last few straws. "How come my mother has not been able to take even a few days out for us and cannot get to the capital for her own son's marriage. At this point none of us even remember how she looks like father!!! O dear Father! All your life you have taken the pains to be both a father and a mother to us. I beseech you to just drop this pretense for her. All she ever wanted is to travel the world on your expense. She has avoided meeting us on all occasions. How is that possible for a mother??? What does that tell you father??? I know she never loved us ever. She never loved me; she never loved you; She never loved any of us." Trilokyachandra wasn't able to find any words that could make his son think otherwise. *Maybe even this was part of her plan... who knows... she never does anything without thinking about it... maybe there is some good in it... sigh... I am getting too old for all this... □*

The queen keeps sending regular dispatches bearing information on various technological, ideological, trade and civil improvements from the court of Emperor Huang. Many of these messages relate to science and technology since such information is relatively easy to get a hold of for the personal physician and royal midwife in the emperor's court. Trilokyachandra sets up multiple schools of science and engineering and to his surprise, is thanked by the emperor to help spread the knowledge throughout the region. Now, there are rumors that Emperor Trilokyachandra, although not of Chinese origin is also being considered for the position of The Protector General of the Southwestern Protectorate of China. Although he never quite makes it to that position, but such news gains him immense prestige far and wide and helps him gain a couple of other provinces without even lifting his sword. These provinces submit to become vassals of the Udabhandh Empire because of its wealth, knowledge, and stability in the region. This results in the Udabhandh Empire becoming the largest empire in the Northern India that also happens to have extremely good relations with Chinese Empire.

Years pass and the young princess is close to coming of age and there already are a lot of suiters that have approached the emperor Trilok for her hand. Vijyavati visits him and offers to teach their daughter different northern languages so that she could visit the court of the Chinese Emperor, gain some prestige for herself which in turn would help Trilokyachandra find an even better match for her. He couldn't have said no, but it pains him daily to see Vijyavati disguised as a poor physician from China trying to teach her fussy daughter different languages. Meanwhile the Chinese emperor asks him to help him with the Mongol raiders. This engages Trilokyachandra in a military conflict for the next many years and takes him far and wide across the Tibetan Plateau and many northern regions he never thought he would visit in this life. All this time, his only consolation was the constant stream of news, from the home front, he would receive every few days and the occasional message from his wife. In the next few years, the princess is able to learn many new languages and visits the Chinese Emperor's court. She is received very well and surprises a lot of people with her brilliance and logical reasoning skills. When she comes back home, her father receives requests for her to be married to the most prestigious houses in India. She is married to the Prince Bharat of Rajputana Empire and yet another alliance is formed between two houses solidifying their position.

All these years of quelling the raiders takes a heavy mental and physical toll on Trilokyachandra. Although victorious, he comes back a tired war veteran and develops an addiction for alcohol. One day while playing the game of javelin throw in almost a drunk state with some courtiers, he blurts out, "Even if he threw the spear on China my wife would be able to catch it and use it to help me!" He realizes what he has said and tries to reverse course but knows that the spies in his court have the wind of this secret now. At once, he sends word to the queen, but she lets him know that she will handle it. In turn, she requests him to control his drinking. Although the emperor agrees, he is not able to control his drinking and found dead in a drunken stupor a few months afterwards. □

Gautamdeva is named Emperor, but there is talk yet again of him not being mature enough to rule such a big empire yet. There are rumors of some courtiers that have ties to the kingdoms of Jumla and Dolti trying to convey potentially devastating information about the queen to the Chinese Emperor. These are early days in Gautamdeva's tenure as an emperor and this concerns him deeply since not only does, he not know where his mother is but also not sure if there is any truth to the rumors.

A few days afterwards, spymaster Chittajeet lets Gautamdeva know that Emperor Huang has dispatched a party consisting of the Protector General of the Western Protectorate along with the emperor's wife to pay condolences for the loss of his father. *How very smart... all you need to come here is to verify the identity of my mother.... How am I going to get out of this now... O Mother! You've ruined us all...* Gautamdeva is shaken out of a stupor by a familiar voice, "Although I have dispatched messengers to the last known location of the queen mother, I would request your highness to allow me to go in search of someone who would match the queen mother's description, in case, the queen mother is not able to make it to the capital before the Chinese delegation." Says Chittajeet. *And you still think you will find her there… either you are an idiot, or you are just pretending now…* "Focus on finding someone. Don't come back without an answer." Chittajeet leaves the capital at once with a party. □

Just days before the arrival of the Chinese delegation a woman comes to visit Trilokyachandra with his old and now retired minister, Satinder Singh. She tells him that she is his mother and has come back from her tour of the kingdom. The timing of her comeback completely surprises him. Although he is enraged to see the woman who left her family for a lifetime of travel, Satinder asks him to keep his temper and prepare for the Chinese contingent that is going to arrive soon. The woman in front of him is quite hideous, with skin burnt at places, maybe from Sun or sweat (he wouldn't know either way). He struggles to match this woman to the last memory of his mother but finds it too vague to help. *Why am I even trying…. It will never work… I have never seen her… and Satinder Singh is here as well… what reason would he have to lie to me… why do I even care… as long as the Chinese contingent can see her here, everything should be good…* "Mother, you couldn't have come at a more opportune time. I will have the guards show you to your quarters."

The very next day, a few days before the Chinese party are to arrive, he is told by his mother's maids that she has been crying all day thinking about his father and is not eating or drinking anything at all. When he goes and visits her, he is told she is mourning her father. He tries to console her, but it is of no use. *...these crocodile tears... this show she is putting up... what does she want out of that... all her life she never cared for us and now this... hah... cry all you want if I care... all I care is you don't die on me soon... otherwise the court is going to blame me for that as well...* "Mother, please stop crying and eat something. I understand your pain, but if you damage your health, it will hurt father's soul even more to see you like that. Please tell me what you need, and I promise I would do anything to make that happen." The woman looks at him through tired and darkened eyes, "My son. I know you hate me for not being with our family for all of your lives. I know you have had to constantly live with the shame of being without a queen when I should have been there. I know how you feel, and I don't hold that against you." *...ok...* "However, you should understand the reason I was away was on your father's orders only. It was him who recognized the best in me and sent me to help out wherever help was needed. He could have forced me to stay in the capital at any time. However, in his greatness, he saw us as partners in building this kingdom and he placed the interest of the empire before his personal interests. We both knew that this would be hard on you and your sister, but that is the true cost of being a king my son. I don't expect you to forgive me, but I hope you could at least understand the reasons behind our actions and how it helped us come from where we started to where you are today." Gautamdeva was silent. He was boiling inside but he knew he had to contain himself. He kept listening "The only thing I will ever ask of you my son is to punish whosoever had spread this mis-information to the Chinese Emperor and caused such a divide between two houses that have been together for decades now." His mother's request somehow hit home. After so many years, all she asked of him is something that would help him become strong. *...is she really telling the truth... was it father who kept her away all this time... no wonder he never answered any of my questions when I asked about her and why he doesn't call her back... I was such an idiot... all this time when my parents were thinking about the country, all I was talking about was myself... and yet... they kept working...* The young emperor felt the pain of a decade in a few moments. He tried to visualize his last memory of his mother on the dinner table, saying goodbye to his father and remembered how much they loved each other... Then he saw all of this drama the result of a small petty king trying to make it big by talking nonsense about his family. *...kingdoms of Jumla and Dolti... just so that you could get into the Chinese Emperor's good graces, you decided to sow discontent between our houses... you tried to take advantage of my father's mistake when he was weak and tired... and now you are trying to undermine my rule...* The emperor is enraged, "Mother, I promise that I will make sure that these people will suffer for their actions." He senses his mother hesitating to say something else. "What is it mother? Please feel free to say whatever you would like to say." The woman is silent for some time *she is quite tired... she should eat something...* "Son, the only way this news could have made it to the Chinese court is if there was a spy there. You should let the emperor know of this as well." *...I never thought of that !!! how careless of me...* His mother's strength seemed to have completely broken down now. She lies down with her eyes closed - tears running down her dry eyes, "May my son take this kingdom to new heights. I love you, my son. Now go." □

Gautamdeva sends out fast messengers to the Chinese Emperor about his will to attack the king of Jumla and Dolti because they have disrespected his mother, him as well as both his house and the house of the Chinese Emperor. He asks the emperor to be on the lookout for spies in his court that have helped spread this information.

As the Chinese delegation arrives in the capital, they are greeted with a country readying itself to go to war. The wife of the emperor Queen Dagmo is told about the state of mourning in which the queen mother is. Queen Dagmo goes to meet the queen mother immediately and couldn't help but sympathize with her for her loss, especially when she had spent all her life outside the palace, enduring all sorts of hardships for the betterment of the kingdom. "Queen Vijyavati, our houses have been joined like family for so many years. Gautamdeva is not only my son-in-law but is also like my own son. I promise you that once I get back, I will ask the emperor to punish those individuals who have dared to spoil the relations between our houses. I will make sure that the emperor also helps young Gautamdeva establish himself as an emperor just like we would help our own son."

Once in her chambers, Queen Dagmo sends messengers to the emperor informing of the false rumors that had been spread in the court and to find out the spy who could be doing that. Seeing that there is nothing left to verify, and that Gautamdeva is preparing for war, the emperor calls the delegation back and sends his blessings to the young emperor as well as assurance that he would support him quash this rascal who tried to put a divide between these two great houses. □

Emperor Gautamdeva marches his army towards Jumla first where is met by a huge force from the Chinese Emperor. The commander informs him that he will assist him to travel and to take over to specific military strongholds of these kingdoms, locations of which, have come to light recently. Gautamdeva wins the war easily and on his way back sends his thanks to the Chinese emperor for sending his troops with specific information that has let them win these battles.

As he makes his way back to the capital, he is notified that the health of his mother has taken a turn for the worse. He hurries back only to find his mother on her death bed since she has not eaten of drunk anything for the last many days. What is even stranger is that his spymaster Chittajeet is sitting on the ground next to the bed and is a state of complete dishevel. As Gautamdeva enters the room, he sees his mother look at him and she is about to say something when Chittajeet calls out the woman, "Mother, please don't speak!!! You are too weak... just rest..." *Chittajeet???!!!* *MOTHER???!!!* Gautamdeva moves towards the bed unable to understand what is going on. The woman on the bed looks at Chittajeet, "Its ok my son. I need to do this."

*...what is going on...* "For my sake... and for your sake..." the woman bows to the emperor with her eyes. "Your highness, I apologize for deceiving you for the last few days. As you would have figured out by now, I am not your mother. I am her maid and I owe her my life because she not only saved my son Chitta from being executed once but also gave him the opportunity to serve his king. She had told me to come here in her place. Everything I said, I said because my queen had asked me to say... as-is... Even... even...", the woman looks up towards the ceiling, "...oh my queen..." Gautamdeva's head was spinning trying to figure out what he was being told. "My king, she had ordered me to convince you to send the missive to the Chinese court regarding the spy. All she wanted to do is to remove even the smallest shred of suspicion from her son – even if it costed her, her own life. That is how much she loved you... your highness..." The woman seems to be retaining her consciousness only by her sheer will to speak. "...your highness... please..." Gautamdeva looks at Chittajeet as the woman in front of him tries to hold on to the last breath and notices the resemblance. "...please... my son... sire... he does not know any of this... it was to ensure your safety... it was how the queen wanted it done... please..." the

woman clenches her stomach and cries out loud. The royal physician standing behind Chittajeet slowly shakes his head sideways, "it's too late your highness." The woman seems to be on her last breath and is trying to speak something. "Mother please keep quiet. Please rest mother. I request you mother!!!" Instead, the woman seems to be trying to get up. She holds on to her son's hand and raises her body just enough to be able to turn it sideways. She barely brings both of her hands forward close to each other; now unable to open her eyes, she takes a few shallow breaths trying to gain some energy to speak. "...please... your highness... please take care of my son... and if possible, forgive me..." her body gives up. "MOTHER!!!" Chittajeet lunges forward to hold her as she drops forward and returns her to her bed. All he could do now is cry with his head near her hands.

Gautamdeva notices a guard with a message in his hand and signals him to come in. The guard hands him the message which is has the seal of the Chinese Emperor.

My dear son,

I am not your father, but today I feel like I should act like one. I knew your father; better than most of his other colleagues. In him, I had found a lifelong friend and I was honored when our friendship turned into family relations. From that perspective, I feel the need to ensure the son of my best friend does well in life. Moving forward consider me just as you did your real father and don't be shy of discussing anything that comes to your mind with this old fellow.

Also, I feel that I should mention that you don't need to thank me for the location of the military strongholds in the last battles. It is due to your missive I was able to capture the Jumla spy in my court. We were able to extract those details from her. I feel I need to thank you instead. Without your missive, I would have never thought of conducting a spy hunt in my court. It was that which spooked this spy to run towards Jumla where she was caught. It turned out to be someone who has worked as our royal physician for so many years and if you can remember, was also in your father's court on occasion tutoring your sister on various languages. It pains me to lose courtier who had been loyal for all these years, but all the information we could extract from her more than made up for it.

With this missive, I am also sending you the claims to all the provinces in the Kingdom of Nepal. Consider this as a gift from a father to son and a little tribute from my side to have burdened your mother when she was in mourning for your father.

Although I consider the case of the spy in my court settled after she provided us all this information and being executed afterwards, I still feel there was more to her than met the eye. The spy did not look like she was from the region of Jumla at all and what she said right before she was executed still confounds me - "Now I am as free as a farmer" Let me know if some day you come to realize what that might mean. Since both the king of Jumla and Dolti have been killed in battle, I feel we have no way to find the truth about what truly happened.

Whosoever, she was, she was the midwife to my first wife when my daughter, now your wife, was born and then a loyal physician who saved our family on multiple occasions. We will feel her loss deeply. I request you to help contain any sort of rumors people might try to spread around her. May, her soul rest in peace.

Health and happiness to your family

a father

Emperor Huang Jingzu

---

Reality slowly dawned on the Emperor Gautamdeva as he fell to his knees in tears... *mother... O Mother....!!!* ∎

# A KING'S SON

Young Dharmaputra could not understand why his mother was so happy today. "My son... You are going to be a king one day." she said. "Go pay your respects to grandpa. Because of his hard work the king has made him a Ngapo. If you work hard like him one day you will be a king!!! Go now!". Young Dharmaputra could not understand what his mother was trying to tell him, but he could surely smell the sweet smell of fresh sweets being prepared and put on different tables for the courtiers to view and taste. He was definitely enjoying this air of festivities, and he ran towards where his favorite person Kanchan Kaka, the head cook was preparing all these sweets. Dharmaputra passed through various rooms being dressed up with flowers, new curtains, and carpets. He knew he took the longer route since he also wanted to hear the various music groups performing in different parts of the castle. He especially liked to watch the part where ladies would be dancing instead of guys, but he had to make sure that his mom didn't see him watching the dance. Today was different though. His mom was too busy to see where he was going. She didn't even ask him if he has completed his daily study!!! *This is how all days should be!!!* A sweet smile spread on the prince's face as a wave of happiness passed over him.

Dharmaputra wanted to find his younger brother Shivaputra before he went to his grandfather. He wanted to make sure that Shivaputra didn't get any extra gifts from grandfather and also to check if he already has got more gifts from grandfather already. *If he has then I will tell grandfather about the extra gift first, because Shiva will not take it to grandfather. I know it!!! He will hide it!!!* Dharmaputra got really frustrated why Shivaputra, the son of the late husband of Dharmaputra's father's sister, Gauridevi, got the same gift as him...

*when he was not even a real prince!!! Everyone knows that already!!! They keep feeding him when he is so big already!!! He should know he is not the prince!!! I am the prince!!! Of course, this should be very easy to understand. Everyone else knows and calls me "Prince". Why HE doesn't get it???!!! Even then he could just copy others... Maybe he's not smart enough to understand this... well that's what you get by not being a real prince. Huh! Next time I am going to ask the servants to explain it to him!!!* As Dharmaputra reached close to his Grandfather's court chambers he heard a familiar voice calling him. It was Meera aunty. She worked for his mom, and he liked her very much because she always gave him sweets and toys. "Dharma, see your grandfather is talking to his friends and advisors on something very serious and he has told me to take you to your new toys when you came here. Let's go to your room. He will come there when he is done with the boring things he does. How does that sound?" *Meera aunty always has great ideas!!! Grandfather is anyways doing his boring things with those other people. He doesn't even have any magicians or jugglers in the court right now.* "Ok, let's go!" As Meerabai offered her arms, the prince jumped up and Meerabai carried him to his room to the order of the Ngapo Prithvipal.

□

Prithvipal who had worked as a Dampati, a mayor, has been handed Ngapoship of Nimisa by the King, Gyalpo Purgyal Yulsung, and although at fifty-two, he was getting old, he had no intention from either backing down from his duties to his kings as well as from this opportunity to rank up his family in royal hierarchy. Ngapo Prithvipal was in middle of a set of meetings with his new courtiers to better understand the dealings of state that he had never tackled before. It was related to various aspects such as defense, development, commerce, culture, etc. in the newly expanded estate that was his responsibility moving forward. Although he maintained an air of confidence and calm throughout the day, Prithvipal knew none of these courtiers would be able to solve his biggest problem.

As his earlier post of Dampati, he would not have inherited any land. He rose to that rank purely based on his own merit. He had helped the city stave off famine many times by his vigilant planning. His sharp eye towards the political situation of the east helped him warn the king of an impending Mongol raid for which the king was able to adequately prepare, thanks to his recommendations and mercenary contracts he helped setup over the months before the raids. Acts of intelligence, bravery and exemplary diplomacy helped him become a constant at the king's court early in his life and a trusted advisor later. That said, none of his family ever planned for the king's generosity.

Prithvipal had one son, Gautamdeva, after his first one passed away at the age of twelve due to an unknown sickness. Gautamdeva, now thirty-six, was renowned for his skill with money. In fact, King Yulsung knew of Gautamdeva's skills very well and had him not only work with the Royal Steward but also sent him on assignments across the country and to neighboring countries, initially to learn as much as he could and later an auditor to various holdings and counties across the country. The focus of Gautamdeva's career was managing finances. He was a world class steward. However, that, Prithvipal knew, would not be enough to manage this land. He knew Gautamdeva didn't have enough martial or leadership skills to be a leader in his own right. *I know he won't like it when I pull him out of all these things, he is busy doing, and start sending him on all sorts of missions to learn all these different skills he needs to learn! I just hope he understands why I am doing this. Sigh... Well, that is the burden of leadership, and he needs to understand this whether he likes it or not!*

After the first few days of celebrations, Ngapo Prithvipal gets the king's permission to pull his son back from the missions he was on in the other part of the country. He then sends him as well as both of his grandsons back to school. The gurus at the school are extremely confused about admitting someone Gautamdeva's age but reluctantly agree when they understand Ngapo's arguments. Gautamdeva is to be given re-training in various martial, political, and diplomatic skills, however, given his age the king allocates special funds and tutors that are called from far and wide to help him train as fast as possible. Dharmaputra and Shivaputra are enrolled in the regular courses designed for training royalty in the affairs of the state.

As years pass, Ngapo learns that both his grandsons are doing well in their education, but much to his chagrin, Gautamdeva seems to be unable to do well in his training when it comes to building muscle memory and fighting skills. He seems to know the ins and out of the theory however doesn't seem to be faring too well on the training battles. He asks Gautamdeva to come to hunt with him however Gautamdeva refuses most of the times making up excuses related to something coming up from his studies at or around the time of hunt. Over the years, not only the Ngapo and his ministers but also, as a trusted friend, the King Yulsung becomes concerned with Gautamdeva's somewhat meager martial skills.

In one of the visits to the King's court, the King suggested that that maybe Ngapo needs to take a stronger action to push Gautamdeva towards become a stronger fighter. Although the king made sure that he spoke to Prithvipal in confidence; this was the first time in Prithvipal's life when he was let know of something he had been tasked to manage and had not gone well. It hurt Prithvipal's ego to the core. He knew the king meant well but is pained by the fact that the situation is not entirely under his control. *Or maybe it is???!!! Maybe I have not been a good commander. I've just been focused too much on administration to influence Dharma towards theoretical pursuits. Maybe it is me who needs to change. If I need to toughen my son, it is me who needs to get tough...* From then on, the Ngapo thought about it during the meetings, and he thought about it during the lunches. The king saw this change that had come over his friend, and he knew very well what it was. He respected Prithvipal to let him be the father he wanted and gave him time to figure it out himself. He had some idea about what should be done one Prithvipal got back, *but it has to be a decision Prithvi would have to take on his own...* it wasn't something he would force his friend to do. A week after, Privipal got back to his court. Everyone was surprised how he seemed to have the energy of a madman. "Call the martial..." he shouted at the captain as he entered the palace, "... and find where Vikrambhatt is..." *ok spymaster... time to earn your pay!!!* □

The next two days the Ngapo was mostly with a very small group of advisors. Even the court was cancelled. When this news reached Gautamdeva, he got concerned and made his way to see his father. As he entered the chamber deep inside the fort, he saw his father standing looking intently at something on the table along with his chief ministers, his marshal, and *this other guy who I know works for my father but not sure what he does exactly...* His father raised his hand towards him without even looking away from the table and with a quick gesture of fingers asked to come closer and look. "Is everything alright father? Mother is concerned that you are not yourself since you came back. Looking at all of you here like this, I am concerned as well..." Prithvipal sighed... *This idiot still doesn't understand what we are looking at in front of him...* He gestures at the map in front of him, "What do you think all this is?" Gautamdeva looks at the table and responds, "It's some sort of battle plan. You are trying to understand strategies to defeat enemy armies if they attack us from the north..." *... at least he is not that dumb...* "... Are we under attack ... or is there going to be one?" Prithvipal looked in his son's eyes. "We are not defending here." Moments of silence followed as the

Ngapo let it sink in the prince's mind. *Yes son... we are attacking.* "This is you with your units – both mounted and infantry. Look at this and now tell me what exactly are we doing here."

The prince could feel his breathing slow down and hear his own heartbeat in his ears. He had never been surprised like that before. He tried to remember all the lessons on army organization in the last few months. He saw his army at a distinct disadvantage of being in a valley and the enemy army at a higher altitude. He tried to think of a way to move around the enemy, but he saw that this was a chokepoint with high cliffs that allowed movement only in a very narrow space. Every time he tried to think of a strategy... any strategy to get to the enemy... he failed with his unit massacred. He looked up towards his father and tried to circumvent the question. "Who are we attacking and why? What problem are we trying to solve?" Prithvipal looked at him as if trying to inspect him from head to toe. "The problem we are trying to solve is in front of you commander! All you need to tell me how to win this engagement."

The prince knew there was no way out of this and

looked back on the map again. His eyes darted from one corner to the other, looking for any attack of opportunity. Any place where there might be a cover... an advantage. He felt the eyes of the whole room were on him. He had to say something. He was sure there was no easy way out. *People were going to die. A lot of people!!! Maybe this was a trick question... this has to be... At once something come to his mind... maybe he is trying to teach the others... maybe this needs to be done with an unorthodox approach... hummm...* The prince ran a few calculations, and he knew this could work... "The only way to move forward is through this narrow gap but we all know this is too risky since the enemy archers would have clear shot to our soldiers as they make their way up the mountain." "So...???", said Prithvipal. "Trebuchets!", said the prince. "According to my calculations, we can install trebuchets on our side of the mountain. This should easily weaken the enemy posts and help us advance while we move our units up the hill. We stop firing when we reach on the other side where we can engage the enemy at melee range. This should minimize causalities."

The prince waited for someone to respond.

Prithvipal kept his eyes on the map while the prince was speaking and then looked at the marshal. He wanted this to be a fair assessment rather than biased by his own views of this strategy. "What do you think Malik Singh?" Malik Singh hesitated and looked at others to judge what they all thought about the plan. "Malik!?? Just say it. What do you think???" The Ngapo ordered. The marshal had no choice left. "Your highness. There are a lot of complications with this plan. At best it could work but still cause a lot of deaths as our armies make their way up the mountain while the stone or fire, we launch at them comes rolling down on our men..." Prithvi looked at the prince who seemed to be listening with his head down. "There is also the problem of setting up the trebuchets on a mountain which has forest on both sides. Even if we manage to setup and fire, the enemy could just move up the mountain and be outside our range and yet cause problems for our armies below."

The room was silent for many moments. The prince spoke, "Yes marshal, I apologize, I did not consider these issues in my analysis." "Please your highness, you don't have to..." "Malik Singh, tell me what would you do???", interrupted Prithvipal. It was Malik Sing's turn. The prince was silent and his breath shallow. He had never seen this side of his father ever. *What has gotten into him today!!! What can Malik Singh tell you here!!!??? Isn't this clear, it's a hard place to fight???!!! Sigh…* The room was quiet. Malik Singh looked up and asked, "Your highness, roughly when do we plan to have this engagement?" "Take your pick. In a couple of months." Malik looked at the board and tried to move a couple of pieces on the enemy side as if trying to create an arrangement. He took a deep breath before he spoke. "We can do this, but we need time. At least six months. And we need to make sure that the path our armies take do not involve more than one such obstacle." "What do you plan to do?"

Malik looked at Vikrambhatt and smiled before turning back to Prithvipal. "Your highness, the prince wasn't wrong in his assessment that a direct confrontation here is going to be costly. For that reason, I would ask my esteemed colleague Vikrambhatt to help me plant some soldier spies in the enemy army." *Huh… neat… I never thought of that… so this is what this Vikrambhatt guy does… he is the spymaster…* "They need to be at various levels so that they can co-ordinate their deployment at this unit when the time comes. Even when that is done, their placement is quite important. We can have them throw vials of poisonous gas in the army ranks that will kill and confuse the enemy from behind while we make our progress upwards. With a fully loaded unit in front of them, it is almost guaranteed that these spies will die as soon as their identities are revealed. Hence the number and positioning of these spies, their training and even finding such people will be a challenge. But I think we can get that done in the next six months or so. Obviously, Vikrambhatt would be in a much better position to say if this is possible or not." Prithvipal looked at Vikrambhatt who merely nodded in approval. The Ngapo then looked at the prince. "I am sorry your highness, I should have thought of a better plan. I will try to explore strategies that involve various non martial tactics in my future studies." At once something snapped in his father. "No!!! Not in your studies!!! You asked what is the problem we are trying to solve. This!!! This is exactly the problem we are trying to solve. You need to get out of your books. Not everything can be in a book and the most important things you will learn will never be in any book. You know why? Because if you wrote them, your enemy could learn of your tricks. You need to get out of your books and go on the field. There are things you need to learn the hard way. And if you cannot then..." Prithvipal took a deep breath and looked somewhere far. "Your highness, please don't be worried, given the prince's high intelligence, he will be able to pick up these things quite quickly.", spoke the Chief Minister Ramdas. "Ramdas! don't defend the prince!!!" Ramdas bowed and stood still. "Gautamdeva, we attack Sravasti in six months. I assign you to train under Malik Singh. Whether you like it or not, you are going to partake in a war soon. All I can say is, Get Ready!" Prithvipal then looked at Malik Singh. "Malik Singh, I am placing the responsibility to train Dharma for the coming battle on your shoulders. If I hear from anyone that you showed Gautamdeva any leniency due to his birth, I would have you and your whole family expelled from the kingdom. Treat him just like any other soldier under your command. He will start from the bottom, and he will have to make his way up. Am I clear ???!!!" Malik Singh was trying to digest this avalanche of orders thrown at him. He was not sure what was possible and what was not. He bowed, "Yes your highness, I will try my best." □

Months went by quickly. Prithvipal kept getting regular updates from his marshal regarding how his son was doing. Things looked promising; well, more promising than before. As the day of the war approached, Prithvipal needed to assure himself more and more that he was not giving too much credit to the prince's performance reports. He was afraid that if he did so, and if he was wrong, he would be willingly leading his own son to his suicide. His encouragement, in that case, would prove to be the poison that keeps his son from becoming a better fighter – something that might save his life and this kingdom someday. *I will have to tough it out... as would my son... it is for his own sake...* It broke his heart many a times to brush off his son a couple of times just to have him understand that flattery will not get him anywhere... *Oh my son... I know you might not mean bad... but I cannot let you become weak now... not now... you must train hard... I hope you will see it one day...* The Ngapo knew the courtiers were thinking of him being too hard on his son, but *I don't care.... He is my son... not theirs... they will just watch... and laugh... they don't really care...*

Gautamdeva's scores looked really good now. He

had improved significantly since the last four months. *Thank you, Malik Singh... I know this has not been easy...* Prithvipal eyes focused on his son... *I know you are trying hard my son... I know... but you need to understand we are going on a war in a month... and you need to be ready!!!* "Gautamdeva... I have reports here that you still need to practice your dueling skills with a sword. Go and focus on those and next time improve on these dueling scores. I want you in your best shape before the next month!" Prithvipal saw a flicker of disappointment in his son's eyes as he bowed and took his leave. *Live long my son... live long...* □

Two months later, Prithvipal was in his camp, on field. He was looking at reports from his commanders that kept him abreast of how the war was progressing. Things were looking well. The spies had done their job well and crossing the ravine did not take long. Ngapo expected skirmishes in the fields that would last at most another few hours before his army would enter the city limits.

From the corner of his eye, he saw one of many messengers slide off his horse and run to Malik Singh with a message. What caught Prithvipal's attention though, was how Malik Singh reacted after he read the message and looked out in the distance... blinking... thinking. As he turned back, he saw his liege looking at him expectantly. He had not fully thought out how he was going to let his Ngapo know about the message. He tried to form a few words but failed. He fell down to his knees and held up the message roll for Prithvipal to read. Prithvipal grabbed the roll with an alarm... His eyes trying to read till the end before his mind could understand the words. He had to read the messages a couple of times before his hands smashed the message on his marshal. "WHYYYYY... ARGGGGHHHH....". Tears welled in his eyes, and he yelled so loud that the entire camp stood still.

Chief minister Ramdas had just come out from his tent. When he saw the scene, he picked up the message and read it silently. He called two captains at once and ordered them off immediately to take care of something. He stepped and bent close to his Ngapo and whispered, "Your highness, although it's impossible, I must ask you to please keep your calm. Hold your feelings until we have won this war. We could have enemy spies watching us and at this time, knowledge of this news could also be dangerous to Dharmaputra. We can absolutely not afford to show our feelings right now my sire." Ramdas then spoke up in an exceptionally stern and loud voice to Malik Singh. "Malik Singh!!! You need to be punished to let that information be stolen and allow enemy assassins to enter our camp!!! We will take care of this once we get back!!!" Malik Singh looked up confused... tears running down his face... "Get up right this instant Malik Singh!!! Attend to your post to make sure that this mistake of yours doesn't cost us much trouble. Now get up!!! RIGHT NOW!!!" Ramdas bent and held Malik Singh by his shoulders "Not right now Malik Singh. Not right now... We will have time to mourn later. We need to protect the kingdom and princes right now. I have already sent two commanders to take the princes into protective custody and bring them back to the palace. I request you to please hold yourself and help us win whatever remains of this war. We cannot let the truth of how the prince died become public knowledge. Think of how everyone will laugh at us. We need to contain this knowledge. The fact that prince had that duel when almost all of the north-eastern forest had been cleared should make it easy for us to clear any witnesses that remain. Even the messenger who brought this message. We need to bury this right now. I will come up with another story about the prince. Do you understand!!!???" Malik Singh seemed to understand and acted accordingly. He bowed, turned back, and started shouting orders around the camp demanding the most current report from the front. Meanwhile Ramdas took Prithvipal who barely managed to walk inside his tent and ordered the guards to move at least fifteen feet away from the tent wall, added extra guards and ordered them to not allow anyone within that circle without his explicit permission. □

Once inside, Prithvipal broke down. Ground gave way below him and he fell on his knees. *Oh my son... oh my poor son... how could you not know how much I loved you... why did you need to go into that duel...* tears came down as the father groaned in agony and tried to find a reason for what had happened. His son had challenged an enemy captain, Bhaskar Sharif, to an impossible duel. The captain had a reputation for being an expert already, but he was known to be merciless as well. He had killed many known fighters in his duels even when he had the chance to leave the field after he had won. Gautamdeva had challenged this captain even after he knew the impossible odds and had suffered a mortal wound to his abdomen. The few who were watching, called the match to end, Gautamdeva took advantage of the captain letting his guard down for those few moments. With a last breath he swung his sword, slashed across the captain's neck, and beheaded him where he stood. He passed away even before the severed head could close its eyes.

"Stupid boy... oh my stupid boy... he didn't want to lose... even at the cost of his life... oh my stupid child... oh... wretched me... it was me who forced him into this mindset... that he had to prove himself... all because I treated him like he never could win in battle... oh Buddha... take me away from this world... why was I so cruel... to my only boy... my son... who wanted to impress me so much that he died for it... oh god... I should rot in hell for this... please take me God... please take me right now...." He felt a hand on his shoulders... Ramdas... "Sire, although I have ordered the guards to stand far away from where we are, I beg you to please keep your volume down... if not for anything then for your grandson... your heir... I beg you... please..."

Prithvipal realized he is sitting on the ground... he looked up... "Ramdas... what will I do now ??? *what will I tell Gautam's mother... his wife... his son???* How will we manage without a prince???" Ramdas helped Prithvipal sit on a bench, "Your highness, God only places burdens on shoulders that can carry them." Ramdas thought for a couple of moments. "Sire, all we can do now is to make sure that our beloved princess's sacrifice does not go in vain. Malik Singh is already working to ensure that there are no remaining witnesses to the event. The prince deserves the honor of a great warrior that he proved himself to be after defeating that monster captain."      *Defeating???!!!*      *DEFEATING!!!???*

*REALLY!!!!???* Prithvipal choked breathless... *Sigh... yes, I know what you are going to do... I know it's important... but how can you act like that in front of me Ramdas... I know what happened...!!!* "Prince Gautamdeva will get state honors for his great victory over the enemy unit that has been pivotal to us winning this war. For the security of our future heir, I will make sure that both the princes are schooled in the palace moving forward, with your permission of course."

By now, Prithvipal was in a daze. He didn't care. He knew he had been too hard on his son. "Sire, there is another thing that I know you would not want to hear right now, but it's important that you do." Prithvipal turned looked up without lifting his head. "Sire, you can punish me for saying this... but..." "What...???" Prithvipal's patience was on razor's edge "... sire, from now on... you need to stop being the best Ngapo, King Yulsung has had till now. You need to make sure our heirs are strong leaders when you have the time to do it. By the grace of Buddha, the kingdom has been doing well and will do even better with Sravasti under your rule. I request you to take care of your health as much as possible now since only you can ensure that our prince can take your place when the time comes. We all need your guidance your highness. Please let us do the rote work of administration and help this kingdom bring up the next leader like one with blessings from the heavens." Ramdas hesitated "... if your highness... umm... brings up the prince from his young age ... your highness would not face as much ..." *say it...!!! SAY IT!!!* Prithvipal's eyes were embers!!! "... your highness would be able to mentor the prince throughout his training to help him become the leader your highness wants him to be..." Prithvipal was fuming... vapor formed around him as he took heavy breaths... *Ramdas...* he looked at the minister in the eye, who immediately bowed down on his knees. *Ramdas... IF...* heavy breaths... *anyone else ... they...* tears... *lost their head ...* silence... *but...* sweat... *I know...* eyes cloud... it's hard to see... *this ... this is true...* shame buries him... *everyone at the court knows how bad I have been... they've just been quite till now... ALL OF THEM JUST WATCHED!!!!* ...Rage... his body throbs with each pulse... he wants to kill... then he wants to die... *ARGHHHH...* "Your highness... plea..." Prithvipal cannot bury his rage anymore... "GET OUT... GET OUTTTTTTT!!!!" Ramdas crawled backwards many steps before standing, bowed, and walked away. A father… lay on ground… reading the last letter from his son again and again… sobbing in silence. ■

# KING'S PRIZE

<u>Important characters</u>

| | |
|---|---|
| Prithvipal | *Thupo of Nimisa and Saravasti* |
| Vikrambhatt | *Prithvipal's Spymaster* |
| Dharmaputra | *Prithvipal's Gandson* |
| Lajwanti | *Dharmaputra's Wife* |
| Shivaputra | *Prithvipal's Widowed Daughter's Son* |
| Kal | *Personal Advisor* |
| Gyalpo Purgyal Mangsung | *King of Nepal* |
| Maharaja Vajrayudha | *Maharaja of the Ayodhya Kingdom* |
| Sahdev | *Finance Minister* |
| Satyachandra | *Head Pujari of Varanasi* |
| Madhuracharya | *Physician* |

In the months ahead, world didn't matter to Prithvipal. He saw people crying but he knew he was the one who was guilty. Days passed… or maybe it was months… with both Nimisa and Saravasti under him now, people called him a Thupo (a Duke) now… he didn't care. Somehow things ran… somehow things happened… there were some reports that looked like someone wanted to attack him, but it looked like Vikrambatt had suggested something that had worked. At least Ramdas never bothered him with that again. Prithvipal, found himself in the gardens more often than not… sometimes thinking… sometimes digging dirt to plant some tree… mostly both… It made him tired… too tired to think about anything… that was his only escape.

One day Prithvipal was too tired after digging a hole and was sitting just looking at the trees in his garden. Further in the distance, he saw Dharmaputra playing with his brother Shivaputra. They were both on a tree on different branches and were trying to shake them to get the tree to drop as many fruits as possible. Prithvipal noticed how Shivaputra's branch was shaking so much more vigorously than Dharmaputra's branch. As he watched the activity play out in front of him, a shiver ran down his spine. *He is too weak!!! He is too light!!!* Prithvipal noticed himself almost running towards the tree when the kids saw him and started climbing down. Shivaputra came down first. On the other hand, Dharmaputra had stopped his attempts to come down from the last branch and was calling him to catch him in his arms when he jumps down from there. "Baba... catch me!!!" *He is too weak... he is too spoiled... Ramdas was right... I can't let him grow like this...* Prithvipal, felt the child jump in his arms as he was still deep in thought. He brought the child down on the ground disregarding all the sounds the child made resisting to come off his grandfather's arms. *I have to start training him... oh god... how much time have I lost... how old is he already!!!* Prithvipal was walking fast, and the boys were running behind him; trying to keep up. Prithvipal knew he had found his purpose. □

Ten years passed in the flash. Prithvipal completely immersed himself in making sure Dharmaputra turned out unmatched in martial skills and physique. It turned out that Dharmaputra also developed interests that aligned with his training since he had tasted utter humiliation during his early years. When young, Shivaputra, who coincidentally, had a bigger body and a heavier built, and thoroughly enjoyed bullying Dharmaputra whenever he could. Dharmaputra started slow making negligible progress which worried Prithvipal to no end. One day, however, Dharmaputra was able to hold himself in a fight against his brother for the first time. At that moment, he understood this is the path he cannot leave.... He will not leave... Ever!!! Victory tasted sweet!!! Now, however, as a young man, he knew, he paid a price for this skill. He knew his brother was attending school learning other "bookish" things, when he was practicing the glorious art of sword fighting and wrestling. His guru had reminded him multiple times to pay attention to other things than fighting skills, but he found all that boring. He knew he could hire other people do to all that work for him. He remembered the laughs he heard at his back when he would not be able to answer something from those subjects, but he ignored all that. He knew they all would respect him *...no... they would need him... all these insects... they would all be at his feet!!!* to do the one thing none of them would dare to do. Win a war!

Prithvipal was old. He could barely stand up straight. His old friend King Yulsung had passed away a couple of years ago and had asked him to guide his son if he asks for any help. That said, the new King, Gyalpo Purgyal Mangsung was quite capable. He knew how good friends Prithvipal and his father were and how much his father trusted Prithvipal's advise. He considered Prithvipal his paternal uncle and, out of respect, even made sure that Nimisa and Sravasti stay out of any trouble. He knew Prithvipal, at his age, was too old to do any real defense if the need ever arose. Prithvipal, by now, considered a master advisor to the kings and emperors knew how King Mangsung was protecting his lands however, he also knew that this generosity couldn't continue forever. He knew it was time to announce his stepping down from the throne and let the prince take charge. He was very well aware though, that this time he might have the very opposite problem he once had before in front of him.

However, thinking that his grandson was safe calmed him. *The ministers have managed the kingdom well all these years... they can do it with Dharmaputra as well... it will give him time to learn. Learning this isn't this hard. He just has to listen to his advisors.* Prithvipal's thoughts went back to Ramdas asking him to lay back and letting them do the rote work while he focuses on family. *I did not treat him well. He worked for me all his life and he hasn't even said a word...* Sitting at his throne, he looked up and saw old Ramdas sitting on his close-to-the-ground seat, talking to a crowd of people, courtiers, businessmen, and scholars. Somehow although everyone wanted to fight with each other, every time Ramdas said something, everyone listened quietly. Prithvipal knew he was a master and realized that the sooner he steps down, the more time Ramdas would have to help Dharmaputra learn the ropes. Prithvipal waited... he wasn't sure if he had slept through it or if the argument was going on just a moment ago... *I hope I did not sleep!!! If I did, I hope no one noticed!!! Did I snore!!!??? In the court!!!??? Oh Buddha... this is high time someone else take this job!!!* The argument had settled and Ramdas looked up at him after he had done taking his notes and sorting his busy table. It seemed like he didn't expect Prithvipal to be looking straight at him. At once he looked at the guards and gestured to them ordering them to let everyone else outside go home. Court was over for today. Prithvipal realized it's been *months ??? or years ???!!!* since he spoke directly to Ramdas other than something that was actively being discussed in court. Ramdas got up and came towards him to help him get up. Prithvipal realized how he had gotten used to this. He even felt ashamed and tried to stand straight. Some joint in his body cracked somewhere and it felt good. Now standing straight he took a deep breath and looked around and placed his hand on the shoulders of his trusted advisor and friend. "I am tired. Let's go home." □

The next two months were full of activity in the palace. There was a festive air counting down to that auspicious day when the prince was going to take the seat of the Thupo. Everyone was ablaze with excitement as the coronation took place. There were gifts ranging from Tibetan horses to exotic swords for the Thupo. This was followed soon afterwards by Thupo Dharmaputra getting married. Finance and trade were doing well before Dharmaputra became the Thupo, but at that time, even the king congratulated him about how unbelievably good the business and economy were doing. "It's like you are blessed by Midas himself!" said the king once.

Years passed and Thupo Dharmaputra now a father to a five-year-old son, started getting tired of doing nothing. His advisors were working like a well-oiled machine. His lands were prosperous and an envy of many other Thupos. There was no shortage of people who wanted to work for the army as they almost always found work and good pay without any major risk to life and limb. Crime was at an all time low. Sometimes he wondered what is he expected to do when everything is somehow magically being handled by his councilors. He tried to take a deeper interest in the ongoing activities of the court but at multiple occasions he found out that he just wasn't able to keep up with the details and had to use some excuse or other to walk out before embarrassing himself. The only thing that he could do to pass time without feeling completely useless was to practice fighting and strategy with his commanders. Over the next few months, he became such an expert, that one day he defeated all his captains and commanders in practice. At that moment it struck him. *This isn't good.... These are my commanders. They lead my armies. I am glad we are not at war otherwise these people would have a hard time keeping their heads!!! I need to do something about it. They need be trained so that they can fight... not pretend to fight!!!*

Things started well, but the Thupo found that it was far harder for the men to keep their pretense up when he was pushing them to their paces. He read reports of people leaving and some of his commanders complaining that all this was a proving a bit too excessive. *TOO EXCESSIVE!!! HOW DARE THEY!!! These men who are turning into potatoes sitting and doing nothing and don't even know how to hold their weapon are telling me that ITS TOO EXCESSIVE!!! Now I will show them what it means*

Next week, Surya Kehar, a very well-known mercenary and his company were invited to the fort. They were contracted to train and recruit people in what some believed to be a new type of army that the Thupo was creating. Within the first month, two captains and their companies were declared unfit for duty and fired. Notices were posted across all major towns about the specifics of the skills that would be needed and tested before anyone would be admitted to the army. The news spread like wildfire. There was talk amongst public about guards and army becoming too soft and incapable and this news was received with a lot of excitement – especially amongst the youth – who couldn't get any jobs in the army since the positions were full for the longest time. Tradesmen couldn't be happier with this change as this meant more security for their caravans. A wave of change spread across the lands. Guards and soldiers now had someone who could take their jobs - the common youth. In fact, there were bi-weekly fights where anyone could challenge someone in the army and if they were able to win three such challenges, they would be accepted into the army. At the same time, any army personnel who got challenged and defeated three times would be declared unfit for duty. It was fair... it was efficient... it made the army better... stronger.... more ready... and Dharmaputra loved it!!! The whole structure of society had changed. Various martial sills and becoming a master in them was now recognized as a purpose in itself. Dharmaputra opened the Academy of Military Arts in the capital and saw students come and join from far and wide. Captains discussed strategy, tactics and tools never seen before. Within two years, Dharmaputra had an army like never was seen before.

However, something... something still didn't seem right. Dharmaputra knew his army is all words and no teeth until they see a real war. He, however, knew that too hard of a target could also break the morale of his army and that would ruin all the work he had done for the last many years. He had his eye on Varanasi – the land that is considered to be the birthplace of Buddhism, but it is also one of the Hindu sites of power as well. *If I could take that, nothing could beat that, as a show of my power... my force... I don't care if Hindus still continue worship there. Its bringing in big trade to all the temples. I don't want to mess that up. But if I can take Varanasi... oh that will show every Rajah in India who they are dealing with. And then... after all... its Varanasi!!! One of the five holy sites of Hinduism!!! The place that, according to these Hindus was created by Shiva himself as well as where Brahma's decapitated head had disappeared in the ground. For them little else is more holy than this... With Varanasi under us, we will probably be one of the most important families in India. But I need to start small. Let my armies taste victory first...* Dharmaputra found himself beside his favorite table with a map of the region. He looked at various locations and the order in which he would approach them. His eyes locked on his target. □

Looking at the rate at which Dharmaputra was focused on his army, Maharaja Vajrayudha was anticipating trouble. However, he did not expect it would be Lakhnau. He was expecting a much bigger attack. Maybe on Ayodhya, where he had his special regiments deployed in secret and told them to stay undercover to not let the enemy know he was prepared. If not Ayodhya, he knew, Dharmaputra would attack Mathura. He knew only these cities were grand enough for his armies. *Lakhnau!!! LAKHNAU!!!???* He could understand that it was next door. But other than that!!! Why??? Why Lakhnau... Everyone knew Lakhnau was a trade and culture hub and had a good amount of money. *But still. With this big an army... Lakhnau was like stomping a mouse with an elephant.* Vajrayudha was caught off-guard. He failed to mobilize his armies in time. By the time he heard of the attack, he knew Lakhnau was gone. The immense wave of excitement it generated in the enemy ranks was palpable across his whole kingdom. People were talking about the "Great army of Dharma" and he hated it. He heard news of defections in all segments of his army to his enemy. Vajrayudha was experienced and knew that he didn't have anything resembling morale at this moment and he couldn't mount a counterattack – no matter how much he wanted it. He burned in rage, but he couldn't do anything but to swallow his pride. Dharmaputra got what he wanted – a taste of fame, victory, legacy for his armies. They had tasted blood and they wanted more.

Dharmaputra's next target was much more ambitious. He attacked Dhoti, Jumla and Kurmanchal in the North one after the other. He then proposed the king a plan to construct a tunnel through the mountains to allow the trade to move south directly from Purang rather than take the long winding and dangerous route around the mountains. The King, Gyalpo Purgyal Mangsung, was impressed and agreed. The king, however, was not foolish. As a potential competitor he knew that Dharmaputra has somehow been able conceive plans that get even praised at the emperor's table. At the rate he was grabbing lands, if Dharmaputra were to challenge his claim on the kingdom the current emperor would have a hard time denying that claim. He knew that he had to be cautious moving forward. He knew what was coming but he also knew such was the fate of kings... to fight... to kill... or to be killed... *You Dharmaputra are not your father... I shall be watching... I am still the Gyalpo!* □

For the next few years Dharmaputra focused on stabilizing his newly won lands. He learned that there were a lot of cultural differences as he moved north from Lukhnau towards Doti, Jumla in the Himalayas. Although he didn't care, he felt that switching gears between his own Buddhist religious beliefs, from the Bön religion in North and Hinduism in the south completely caught him off guard at times. He found himself being counselled multiple times in a week on various idiosyncrasies of different religions and things he needs to watch out for. *All religions are welcome... I don't care who you worship...* if he was ruling that region, all that mattered was that it was stable, both financially and from a law-and-order perspective. After ten long years and many deaths he had to explain away as the wrath of the mountain gods, he was finally able to reroute the trade routes through the newly completed tunnels. That however, brought a different set of problems he had not expected to handle.

As the trade caravans moved across the old circuitous route, goods changed hands many times and by the time they entered his lands they were mostly being carried by people who knew the customs and the culture of these lands quite well. The new shortcut created an influx of these traders who used to worship deities that were quite different from those that Buddhist worshipped. Hindus from the South were used to trading with the Buddhist. They would ask their Buddhist friends and partners to help them understand the Bon religion and culture but never really got a good explanation. This confused them and slowly created an atmosphere of distrust when dealing with traders from North. Although on face all traders would pretend to not care and call "business is business" but under the covers a feeling of unease slowly set in. Incidents mostly related to people not cooperating with each other at the borders start being presented to Dharmaputra frequently and this confused him even more. *All this clutter these traders are causing... just do your damn business and be happy. Every day... these stupid people fight for stupid things... who cares if a ceremony is done at one time or the other... who cares if you mark one symbol on the wall for protection or the other... if you don't even make the trade... there is nothing to even protect... since when have these traders become so dumb !!!??? argh...*

Dharmaputra felt that this new development is going to stretch his plans to take Varanasi. *I need to sort these problems out first... but my men... the recruitment is at all time high... so is morale... They need something...* His eyes caught the reports in front of him. He saw the numbers that showed how many trade caravans were coming in and going out. He noticed that the number coming in was much bigger than going out. *Of course... we have become the economic hub in the region...* he smiled as he reminisced about his climb to where he is now. And then it struck him. *All these problems with traders... it's because we are not going outside enough... we expect others to learn who we are... we never go out and learn who our partners are...* He called his finance minister, Sahdev, at once and asked why that was the case. "Sire, even if we wanted to send more caravans out, we can't. Most families here are in the business of buying imported goods and trading them forward for goods that make their way to other big cities such as Mathura and Varanasi. If, however, you are interested in details, I would add that our neighbor to the south, Bharauli buys copious amounts of goods from us at a high rate because they are next door to Varanasi. If it was somehow possible, maybe by making some sort of trade agreement, a lot of traders from there would be willing to go up north to buy good. However, since they would get back to Bharauli, it wouldn't benefit our markets with the cultural and religious knowledge that you seem to be looking for." All this time Dharmaputra was looking at Bharauli. *Right next to Varanasi…. should have a big population of traders ready to go up north….* He tried to do a bit of calculation in his head but gave up after a few moments. *If we owned Bahrauli, and can no longer add "export" charges, we will probably take some loss. But since they sell to Varanasi, we can raise prices there and make a good profit there. Plus… its right next to Varanasi!!!* Looking at Dharmaputra's eyes, the minister could almost anticipate his liege's response. He was concerned that this might be getting too close to Varanasi – the place all Hindu Rajahs could be called to protect if needed. *It was playing with fire.* "Sire, we can look westward as well…" Dharmaputra raised his hand to tell him he has heard enough. "Sahdev, after what you have seen what our armies can do, are you still scared?"

The minister tries to search for a logical response to correctly express his concern. "Sire…", he moved closer to the map, "… its right next to Varanasi…"

he looked in Dharmaputra's eyes, "… the Pujari who heads it… he can…" he waved his hand over the whole map. "…he can call every Hindu Rajah to their defense… every one of them…" Looking at Dharmaputra he asks, "Do you think we can take all that??? You know very well that every one of them will come. To defend the very center of their religion…." Silence… "Who won't???… Am I scared??? Sire, we have some problems… some new problems… it's just traders… we can easily tackle those… are they worth the mountain of death and destruction that attacking close to Varanasi can lead???" The minister was silent, but Dharmaputra knew his answer. He had so much hoped he could get one step closer to Varanasi and solve the trade issue as well in one swoop, but he knew that the minister was right. He will have to figure out a different solution to this problem. □

For the next few days, Dharmaputra couldn't focus on anything happening in the court. Everything was boring *useless... all these quibbles... petty stuff that should be obvious... these people... sigh...* he paced up and down the fort looking at the horizon, seemingly in a sort of trance. Evening came and he still did not have a solution to the problem. He knew discussing with his ministers would only get back the same reply. "He should look West. Stay away from Varanasi !!!" *these people would yell that at my face... what do they know about legacy. They are just employees of the court. All they get to do in their lives is have kids and bring them up. They never get to even think about these things... How will they even come close to understanding what I am thinking...*

When Dharmaputra looked up, he saw he had somehow led himself in the drink house. There were a couple other courtiers in the room enjoying the live music and dance. They sat on their comfy seats and bounced to the beat of the music. The lady at the bar, Zeenabai, looked expectantly towards him, "Something strong... and I don't want any headaches tomorrow... something that helps me think." Zeenabai set to work mixing a flurry of drinks together while the Thupo tried to find a seat for himself. *far away from all this noise... and people... and activity... and light... I just need quiet... I am tired...* somehow his feet found a good location and he slumped in a corner... his eyes heavy... *my head is heavy... I am sleepy as well... I am so tired...* Zeenabai came over with the drink and started saying something to cheer up the Thupo when he gestured her to be quiet and go away. Zeenabai signaled something to the musicians on the other side of the room and in a few moments the music in the room seemed to have lowed itself in volume. The lights dimmed and dance became *less noisy... thank you !!! thank you!!!* Dharmaputra could do nothing but look at his cup.

He imagined the day he will be victorious over Varanasi. *Probably that would be a good day to declare him as a Gyalpo. I can't stand him anyways... I don't know how father worked with him so long... "Gyalpo needs this... Gyalpo needs that..." oh he is a baby in an old body... he probably knows this already... I bet he is waiting for me to call him out on that one day...* His focus shifted to current reality... Bahrauli... he found another person sitting opposite to him. *I have seen him.... Somewhere... I know I saw him at the court... but I think he is also working for some department... I think I rewarded him once...* He tried to remember... *for something... for something really good...* He tried to think what had this person done... *Nothing... argh... this drink...* He slowed his breathing... thought hard... *I think he is one of our top spies... I think he told me something that was true... something that I liked... yes... I think something like that...* As Dharmaputra came out of his thoughts, he found this person to be looking directly at him. He raised his glass, "May God grant our lord..." tipped his head and raised his glass, "... wisdom beyond his age and age beyond count..." Dharmaputra smiled *he knows how to talk...* Dharmaputra raised his glass to him "Health and prosperity to you as well... Have... I have seen you before... right? I just cannot recall." The man bowed slightly, "Sire had sent me to sort out the problems with the missing supplies at the northern junction." Dharmaputra remembered, "Ah yes... and the whole thing had blown up into a mess. And you had sorted out the whole thing... and from what I was told using wise words... and some very well-placed items..." he smiled as he said, "and well-timed confiscations... Yes, I remember you now... Kal??? Kal was your name, right?" "Yes, my lord, I am truly honored that you remember!" "Oh, come on, its nothing. What you did then is worth remembering." Kal bowed again slightly. "All by your grace sire." He looked up and took a sip. "You look tired my lord. Generally, the court keeps you too busy to give you a chance to relax here at this hour." Dharmaputra Kept looking in his drink. *I do feel tired. I have been walking all day. All this thinking... he takes a deep breath. And I can't even talk about it without sounding a greedy maniac. Sigh. Seems like I am all alone on...*" "I am assuming the minister Sahdev was not particularly co-operative..." □

Dharmaputra's eyes focused on this individual. *How does he know...* "Worry not my lord. I did not mean to concern you; only to help. I spend a lot of time with the Minister helping him with executing daily affairs. I could tell something was wrong this morning when Minister came back after meeting you. He kept calling for solutions to solve the trader problem. We all have been up on that since today morning sire." Dharmaputra's shoulders relaxed, "I see... So did you guys find any solution?" "Not yet my lord." Someone came over and filled Thupo's glass. The wine had small bubbles he had not noticed before... Kal spoke as he stirred his drink, "but... somehow, I feel... that is not the question you are looking to be answered..." Silence. Thupo realized his hands had stopped swirling his drink. *This guy... how does he... Let me see what he knows...* He looked at Kal. "What do you mean?" Kal put his drink down. "Sire, I am but a mere child compared to the wisdom of my sire..." He bowed slightly. "... however, it is not hard to see what our sire desires..." Kal paused to choose his words, "I have a certain skill... it allows me to listen to what is not being said... If sire were interested in merely ending the trade disputes, we could have also looked westward at other Hindu trade centers. Sire, I am a weak person by built and know I cannot join the army but that has been my dream since I was born. I simply cannot state how much I love the way you have organized the army. How fair you have been in making sure everyone gets a chance. Although I know I can never be fit to be a soldier, in my mind, I consider you as my mentor and have followed every piece of text on martial skills and strategy in the schools you helped open. I wanted to make sure that if ever the time comes, I am there to help my liege in any situation where I could apply my mind to solve a strategic challenge...." Silence.

Dharmaputra was stunned. This was totally unexpected. "My lord, I know why you chose Lukhnau first instead of anywhere else. It was because you wanted to give our armies some real experience and not only that, you also wanted to make sure that their morale is always high. You looked north to give us the extra land and trade to help with the next stage of your plans." *Which is...???* Kal gestured to a servant standing nearby to go away. "The trade issue is nothing. If I might be a bit bold, I would say that this would just be the second sparrow you want to kill with the same arrow." *...ok...* "My gut sense tells me, that arrow, is pointed to squarely at...” he lowered his voice... “... at Varanasi...” His eyes met Dharmaputra in which he saw the fire that said, “You know I am right!!!” *he is sharp...I must give it to him... How come none of my ministers think like him...!!!???* “If you think that is the case, then what do you think is the problem and how do we solve it?” Kal took a deep breath, sat back, and looked at his drink. “Sire, we both know what the problem is. Since I understood, what you really wanted for the last many months, I have been thinking of a way to solve that problem.” “... and ???” Thupo couldn’t hold himself back. He never expected to find a solution to something he has been banging his mind on since today morning. “Sire, all I can say is that it must be my utter lack of skill that I have been able to find only one solution to this problem and I don’t like it at all.” *What....!!! There is a solution!!!???* Thupo stared him as if asking, “Say it!!!” but Kal kept quiet. *Oh come on.... Say it !!!... SAY IT!!!* “SAY IT!!!...” The room got silent.

Dharmaputra collected himself and gestured for the music to resume. “What is the solution?” “Sire, I am afraid, I am going to die once I even utter it.” *Well...* Thupo cocked his eyebrow, “You will surely get hurt if you don’t tell me about it now that we have spoken about things at this level. I give you my word, no harm will come to you no matter what you say right now." Kal remained silent for a couple of moments. His eyes showing the various choices of words and phrases going on in his head. "Just say it... it's ok. You can be direct about it." At that point Kal seemed to pause. "It's about relationships. You need to build a relationship with the pujaris of our 'place of interest'... but... not just any ordinary relationship. One in which they trust you that at under no circumstance will you ever attack their city. And there is only one way to do that. Well even if it's just one way, it's not easy. And it's not that quick as well..." *he is just rambling now...* "Come to the point!!!" "Sire..." he took a deep breath, "...You have to..." *gulp...* "become a Hindu!!!" □

Kal did not speak further. *He is not joking...!!! He is serious !!! but....* Dharmaputra could feel blood rushing around his eyes and an intense tightness gathering in his belly. ... *what will the rest of the cities think... how will this impact everything else...* "But sire, just becoming a Hindu is not going to be enough. You would need to show the Pujaris your devotion.... Make big donations, invite them for religious ceremonies... You would need to let them understand how a unified land with Bahrauli under you would help them with better goods and trade. Maybe even grant some of their sons, positions in some of your cities. Over time, you would need to have them understand why having Varanasi under your control would be much better for their future, the future of the city and overall, for the Hindu religion... Sire, you need to become the shining example of what a Hindu ruler should be. Today everyone knows you as one of the most righteous rulers in these lands... I know it would not be too hard for you."

This was too much for Dharmaputra and his head was spinning. It made sense to him as he listened to it, but he was imagining the mountain of work he needed to do. *I haven't even started in earnest yet... the first step is already a mountain... ok... hold on... do I want Varanasi that bad!!!??? Ummm... I don't know... I am not sure... OF COURSE I WANT IT!!! THAT IS ALL I HAVE EVER WANTED!!!! ... ugh... I don't know... it's so hard...* "It's hard sire... it's very hard... but the first step is the only one that is this hard... after that all you need to do is entertain these corrupt pujaris and feed them your logic until they get it. After the first step... it's just talk... quite an easy price to pay for what you have wanted for so long." *I know... but to change the religion of my house!!!... no one would like me... no one would trust me...* "Sire, you don't need people to like you. You need them to follow you. With the systems you have created they follow you because the way you have setup things... these systems work for people... that's why they follow you. Not because you are a Buddhist. And if that was the case, then the northerners and the Hindus would already hate you... so in that case what is there to lose??? you lose some you gain some... Once you have Varanasi, you can do whatever you want. You could stay a Hindu if you wanted. Or if you really wished to go back you could do that as well establishing the city where Buddhism was founded back under Buddhist rulership. You would be a hero no matter what you do…"

Dharmaputra seemed to have calmed down a bit. "However, that being said, once you switch to Hinduism, you will see how easy things become for you. Especially if you wanted to expand in the south. The corruption that infects our Hindu lands today would provide you the perfect opportunity to set yourself as an example of The Perfect Ruler. People would love you for that. And selfishly, as a proud Hindu myself, I dare say, you would love being a Hindu yourself as well and probably find going back to Buddhism harder than you thought." He smiled and added, "But I am running ahead of myself here…"

Dharmaputra's mind was already thinking of the impact of such a decision. Somehow Kal spoke his thoughts. "Think about what could happen… when you announce the change, there would surely be people who won't like it… Let's say your advisors… Let's say, in the worse scenario some leave… so what… you have been rejecting so many applications over the last so many years… you could always find someone else…. That said, when most advisors would see that now that you have provided a safety net to the lands from religious attacks from Hindu Rajas, they would see your decision in a different light. The smart ones would understand... and that's what you need..." Dharmaputra had never felt this rush since the last so many years. He was trying to slow himself down. He knew he shouldn't be rash. He also knew the logic was sound. What Kal said was true.

*There is no other way...!!! Buddhism is close to Hinduism anyways... I could always say I started reading ancient texts and now I appreciate both... and when the Pujaris ask... I will tell them how I wanted to go back to the roots of ancient Hindu religion... How the ancient Vedas have opened my eyes. Probably a couple of positions in some mandirs for their kin. They will understand... My family... they know me... they know I only care for the kingdom... they know religion is something on the side... they won't care... I mean... they will care... but they know what really gives them happiness... all this... their positions... as rulers of these lands... and they know... yes, they know!!! I think they know... they should know... that progress needs sacrifices... and when they understand why I am doing this... when they see themselves ruling over*

*Varanasi one day... they will understand... They will...* "Meet me tomorrow morning..." Dharmaputra said as he got up and walked out... "we have many things to plan..." *how am I going to sleep tonight!!!* □

Court was cancelled next day. Dharmaputra sent word that he was too busy investigate something he has just discovered. The palace was abuzz with whispers of some impending announcement. Everyone took a guess. Most pointed to where their Thupo will attack next. The commanders drilled and made sure their units were ready to go in case they were asked just that. Dharmaputra asked for his food to be brought to his study that evening. Lajwanti, Dharmaputra's wife, came to check if everything was alright and found her husband almost buried under a pile of open books and texts all strewn across the room. Dharmaputra's eyes went back on the books once he saw her enter the room.

She had never seen him reading anything with such fervor and she felt quite proud of her husband. She didn't feel like stopping him but was still curious about the change. "My love, I hope everything is alright. I have never seen you so busy with all these books. I know I can't understand all the things you need to do, but I just want to make sure if you are ok and need anything." Thupo looked up. *Oh… he looks so tired… what is it that he needs to work on…* He held her by her shoulders. "Laj, if I had known all these years, what I know now, I would have done this much earlier... I will tell you what I am doing but you need to promise me not to tell anyone else." Lajwanti, was tongue-tied. She wanted to know but didn't know what to say. She nodded. Dharmaputra put his figure on the map and circled on an area. "You wanted to make sure I am safe right... ??? that we are all safe...???" She kept listening. "Well, I have found the answer to that..." She looked at his face. He turned towards her... his eyes lit. "I have come to know of a weapon of the Gods!!!"

She didn't know if he was joking. Her face would have given that away. "Well, just to be clear, I am not saying I found the weapon. All I am saying is that I have found that it exists and is in this area." He circled the same area he circled earlier. "From what the scholars tell me it's the same weapon that Shiva used to behead Brahma once – His fingernail!!! From what is written, it's a weapon of infinite power and there is nothing in this universe that can stand in front of it!!! Imagine, if we have that weapon, we won't need to fight anymore. We can live peacefully, once for all. I will be safe... you will be safe... our children... all of us... will be safe...

forever... because we won't need to fight anymore." Lajwanti couldn't believe what she was hearing. *Has he gone mad!!!??? How come no one else has spoken about this ever before!!!???* "I know what you are thinking... how is this not been ever thought of before... right??? How is it that I am the first one to find this ???" *right... how???* "Well, it's not. We've just never heard it before. Because all we speak of in our court are Buddhist philosophy whenever we ever speak of anything religious. Every Hindu king knows about it and wishes that they would find this weapon. However, there is another reason - they don't have the lands we have – Other than Bharauli and Varanasi, this area includes mostly all the lands we have so they can anyways not get here. Most of them... their great grandfathers... and even before those... they just gave up. We on the other hand... never even knew !!!" His eyes met his wife's. *I am doing what you have always asked me for – I hope you understand this.*

Lajwanti being from a Hindu family, could see his logic. *It's about searching something anyways... sure... search as long as you want...* She looked at the map. "So how are you going to search Bharauli and Varanasi? We don't own those..." The Thupo became a bit serious and looked down on the map. "You are not going to like this." *Huh...* "What do you mean??? What are you going to do???" Her husband's silence was deafening to her. "Tell me!!!" He looked at her and sighed, "...Its only for our family I would do this..." *what is he planning!!! Is he going to attack these two places as well??? Why is he acting like this ??? it cannot be an attack... he has done that before... he has never said this before... O Buddha... I hope he is not planning anything crazy...!!!* "Tomorrow morning..." *what tomorrow morning???* She tried to remember anything unusual she might have noticed in the servants preparing for tomorrow. She didn't. "... We'll become Hindu." *WHAT!!!!* Her eyes bulged!!! Her heart skipped a beat. She forgot she had to breath. "Are... You... ???" she couldn't find a word. *WHAT THE HELL!!!!* She didn't realize she was moving backwards. Dharmaputra moved towards her and held her. "My love, believe me... we need to do this for our children. Otherwise, no matter what I do... they will always be under the threat of death from everyone that surrounds us. Whether it's when we are here or after we are gone. If you really want us to be safe... you will think about it..." She couldn't believe what she was hearing... "Sit down." She felt her being guided down to a seat. Her brain was numb. "I know it's too much to think about. I know it's not right." She kept looking down. *Should I run away with the children!!!??? Or should I kill myself and the children!!!???* "I know right now you are thinking all sorts of crazy things. Your eyes tell me at least that..." Words seemed to bounce off-of her. Dharmaputra shook her to bring her back. He knew he was losing her... *I need to give her something... otherwise this will never work...* "Laj!!! Listen!!! Don't think anything crazy. You can keep being Buddhist secretly!!!" He shook her again, "Don't you see, this is just to convince the pujaris to allow us to search those lands... We won't even need to fight. We will all be safe... like you have always wanted. You can practice whatever you want in secret until we find what we are looking for." *Ok she is breathing now... this is working...* "Don't you see... this is for our kids... would you rather have them die ??? is this too big a price to pay for that ???" He remained silent. He slowly let go of her and bent down in front of her on the ground. He looked up at her, "...is it too much to ask for our kids???" She looked at him. Her eyes were cold. *But she is listening at least...* "You are their mother... you take care of them just like you want. All you need to do is pretend in court.

Stay with me my love. For us and for our children. I am trying to get what you asked of me. It's not easy but it's not impossible." Tears well up in her eyes. Dharmaputra holds her by her chin, "Will you help me do this for our children??? Please..." She nods silently. "...Please for me... for our kids... please stay with us... please don't do anything crazy... we need you... it's all for us... otherwise it's not worth anything... I need you my love..." He looks in her eyes. There is compassion – Maybe for the kids... maybe for him - he does not know – or *maybe she is just overwhelmed and needs support now...* As he takes her hand and kisses her and slightly holds out her arms, she falls over her shoulder in his embrace and weeps.

He gently moves his hands over her head, "It will be over soon my love... not long... we'll get through it... we'll have to be strong... I'll be with you all this time... right here... like always... I would need your help to take care of the children... would you help me with that ???" he feels her nod on her shoulder "...oh my love... I am sorry... I know this is cruel... but we need to do this... I hope you forgive me for this... my queen.... I love you... know this... always..." he hears a faint whisper, "me too..." He

could no longer feel her sobbing... *she is calm....
now to tackle the court...* a hint of smile crosses over
his lips. □

The next day in court was highly unusual. People couldn't make why there was an Agni-Kund, a holy fireplace, typically used in Hindu rituals, in the middle of the court. At the start of the court, twenty-one top brahmins from various places stood in a row in front of a row of Buddhist monks. The court quietened down as the Thupo entered and took his seat. Once all were seated, Dharmaputra started recounting a tale in which on one of his recent adventures in the Himalayan mountains Lord Shiva had appeared in front of him. This caused a huge buzz in the court, however, the Thupo continued. He told the court that he has been instructed by Shiva himself to change his focus to a life of deeper spiritual investigation, reading and public service. From this day onwards, although he will welcome all in his court, however, as instructed by the Lord Shiva himself, he will devote himself to the ideals of Hinduism and explore the deeper meaning of life and spirituality. For this reason, he has invited Hindu Brahmins to help initiate him in his newfound purpose as well as Buddhist monks to bless him in his journey moving forward so that he can help balance the Buddhist culture with his Hindu duties moving forward.

This confused almost everyone except the Hindu Brahmins, who had been told explicitly what they had to do (and they had agreed to) before they were brought in the court. The Buddhist monks on the other hand tried to reason with the king about the change of religion, but he reasoned back with them on the principles of self-exploration as well as being true to oneself. That according to him was the guiding principle and that is why he wanted the Buddhist monks to bless him as well. Although the monks were confused, they felt forcing someone into a religion also violated some of their core principles and helping someone on a spiritual journey was something they could not refuse anyone.

The Thupo got himself initiated by the Brahmins through a holy initiation ritual, Yagya, performed on the Agni-Kund and got his blessings from the monks as well. A few days afterwards, Dharmaputra sent out a party with a hundred cows as a donation to the head pujari of Varanasi, Satyachandra, asking him his permission to visit him for his blessings and to be able to become a member of the society Satyachandra heads. Both Satyachandra as well as Vajrayudha were astonished when they heard the news, although Vajrayudha didn't take this news on its face. He knew that now that Dharmaputra is Hindu, other Hindu kings, including Vajrayudha wouldn't be able to declare a religious war on him. Although he considered that a smart play, he couldn't fathom all the negative repercussions that Dharmaputra could face and might or might not have thought about. *No one I know has done something like this before. I shall wait on how this plays out...*

Pujari Satyachandra permitted Dharmaputra to visit him and had a discussion with him on his recent change of mind – a discussion in which the Thupo was able to thoroughly impress the Pujari of his intentions to learn as much as possible about the depths of Hindu religion as well as the spiritual nature of the universe through his quest that has been given to him by no one else but Lord Shiva himself!

In a few days though, on the home front, things didn't look too well for Dharmaputra. Many of his courtiers left the court on the grounds that he is a heretic, and they cannot stay in his court anymore. After a couple of months, even his personal physician left with an excuse that he has been called to a monastery for a different assignment. Dharmaputra knew that the assignment was just an excuse to get away. Although he was glad to not have a physician who did not like him either.

As Kal had predicted, he did not have too much trouble finding good and sometimes even better replacements for the positions that were left vacant. He found a world-renowned physician for himself as well. The best part was that this physician, Madhuracharya, was a staunch and learned Hindu and also helped him decipher complicated texts that he could quote around to show how much he respects Hinduism and takes his studies seriously. He also administered a strict regime of activities for him to keep him in shape such as weekly hunts with his dog, Shera. Initially Dharmaputra felt that to be a bit overboard but soon stopped complaining as he found it helped clear his mind of the problems in court and gave him a chance to demonstrate his preference to courtiers on who he asked to accompany him on the hunts. Overtime, his hunts increased in duration from a few hours to a few days to a few weeks, when he would go on hunt for mystical creatures said to have seen in his lands.

All this time, he also worked with Kal to move his plan forward step by step. In the next two years, his contributions to the Satyachandra's society increased significantly. He setup a lot of Hindu temples and schools in his lands and contributed generously to Brahmins and on celebrating Hindu festivals. Then as Kal had suggested, he lightly brought up the topic of helping Varanasi become more secure, during a discussion with Satyachandra. Although the pujari hesitated to move into this discussion, Dharmaputra pressed that unless someone with the strength to defend against the Northerners helps reinforce Bahrauli, Varanasi will always be open to exploitation and attack. He intentionally didn't press the Pujari too much on the topic, however, as per Kal's suggestion he helped put spies around the Pujari so that he could help channel his thoughts from being opposed to the idea to being unsure about it.

In a discussion two months afterwards, Dharmaputra brought up the topic again and asked, "I am not asking you to help me win the war. All I am asking my guru is if he would have any problem if I could help Varanasi be more secure than it is today." At that point, Satyachandra couldn't say no. He had not seen the same devotion from Vajrayudha ever before as he had seen from Dharmaputra in the last three years. *Whether he wins or loses shouldn't be my concern: We are priests... we don't think about wars... we are servants of God... as long as there is someone to protect the city of God, all should be good.* "All I care is for Varanasi to be more secure." Was Satyachandra's response. Nothing could make Dharmaputra happier!!! *Kal's plan has worked!!!... Is working!!! This guy is a genius!!!* □

By now, although the Thupo had a council, he would use it only for administrative purposes. He would consult with Kal for any of his planning and when he was convinced what needed to be done, he would just convey his orders to his council to somehow manage them. That said, he had not found any issue with how things were running – none of his council had complained of his orders being difficult, out of line or strange. In fact, what Kal had suggested a few weeks ago was something that his advisor had also brought up in the meeting a few days ago. Dharmaputra had discussed his intent of capturing Bharauli in secret with this chancellor and let him know that Satyachandra from Varanasi would not be opposed to that. In fact, once he has Bahrauli, and has support from Varanasi, Dharmaputra would be able to declare himself the Gyalpo (a King) and challenge the current Gyalpo himself. Although his chancellor was surprised to hear that, he also expressed concern that him holding too many lands by himself might make him seem power hungry as well as take too much of his time and effort in administering the realm. The chancellor had suggested that he could consider granting the Ngapoship of Jumla to his cousin Shivaputra. "Since Jumla is mostly snow all around the year you aren't giving away something that is of tremendous importance. Moreover, since it is also beset by social tension due to the cultural issues, it will take all of it off your worries. This way you can also impress your generosity on Shivaputra and have him take care of all these issues for you. Shivaputra happens to be an excellent administrator and negotiator and probably well suited to something of this nature where a lot needs to be constantly sorted out to keep order." To Dharmaputra, this was killing multiple birds with one arrow. He also made it seem like he never thought about it before with Kal but that it was an original idea from the chancellor. By giving Jumla to Shivaputra, he also would be able to gain trust from his chancellor who now thinks that his liege listens and respects his opinion.

The royal astrologer provided the auspicious date and Shivaputra was granted the Ngapoship of Jumla on the chosen day. As his chancellor had suggested, Dharmaputra felt now he can take the worries related to Jumla off his mind. This was time to focus on Bahrauli – One step away from his lifelong dream – Varanasi. He discussed the strategy he is going to use to approach Bahrauli in detail with Kal. In order to shield himself from other kings getting infuriated by his stepping one step closer to Varanasi, he decided to play the Savior of Hinduism. He sent out his spies in the neighboring kingdoms and have them spread the message that the people of Bahrauli are sick and tired of Vajrayuddha's oppressive rule. "People are unable to practice various Hindu rites as they cannot afford even simple objects, due to the excessive taxes imposed by the king." Within a few months, stories of the king as being one that was greedy to the point of almost hating the Hindu religion, started popping up. The plan was working well. Vajrayudha's forces had weakened due to many soldiers leaving and him having to spread his forces across his lands to quell any riots.

Dharmaputra asked for an auspicious date to be chosen to attack Baharauli. He was told it was exactly a week from today. He had done this many-a-times before. The sequence of events that would follow were at the back of his hand. An almost meditative affair *that helps me forget all these mundane things in the court. For the next few weeks... I can do what I like again... be where the fight is...* He tries to smell the would-be-smell of cannons and gunpowder. In his mind, he hears the hooves and neighs of war-horses and messengers bringing news from the frontlines. *The forces would be ready in about four days. Two days to make any last-minute preparations and then we go. Then there are about two days of marching and then on the third day we fight. The actual fight shouldn't last more than a day. Maybe two to three weeks of sieging the city. Oh, those are fun times... out in the fields... with my captains... late night discussions about war strategies... and then... in a few days.... that's it... the city would be ours... then would start the usual routine to rehabilitate the city... to setup broken homes... businesses... temples... well the ministers would be able to see to that... I would be with my captains... trying to understand and planning and setting up city defense and recruitment. It would be glorious!!!* Looking out of his window that evening, he imagined Bahrauli at the horizon. One day he would be standing in Varanasi. *That day I could rest.*

□

Wee hours of the next morning and the castle was abuzz with activity. The armies were almost ready to leave. But there are always those last-minute things. Dharmaputra woke up to a distant order given to one of the companies. The window was open and chilled morning air filled the room. Lajwanti was already up and busy preparing his carry things. He tried to take in the stillness outside between moments of noise around him. The smell of food being prepared mixed with the burnt smell of newly forged weapons being distributed and carried around in the courtyard excited him... the thrill of battle... *of adventure... of victory... oh how long have I been waiting for this....* He wanted to dream how much fun it would be, but he did not want to miss these moments. A slight smile crossed his lips... *let's do this...* He was a man with a purpose. The attendants knew exactly what to do as he walked towards his bath house. Like clockwork things clicked. He walked to the armor room right after. All these years of practicing ... his body was as rock ... he saw Lajwanti look at him as he got dressed... he saw her smile and press a figure on his rock of a chest... he smiled back... then at once she turned sad and looked in her eyes... "come back soon my love... I will miss you... how will I spend these days without you…” Dharmaputra lifted her chin and gently kissed her on her forehead. “…just a week my love… just a week” and he took her in his arms.

Energy coursed through his body as he came out to the courtyard. Bold and resolute he looked at his commanders and their eyes told him they were ready. He looked back at the captains standing behind… Each chiseled to perfection. *My comrades… I wish I could tell you how important this fight is… I wish I could tell you the all the details… yet…* He looked at them looking back expectantly… “We are all brothers … brothers of this land… brothers united in a single purpose… to make this land… the land of justice… of opportunity… and a land where evil thinks twice before knocking. It is because of us, our mothers… our sisters… our children can walk free without fear… they walk with pride… They know… their husbands… their sons… brothers… that this band of elite warriors have not been seen in hundreds of years… one that is feared across the entire region is here to defend their liberty and freedom of their countrymen. To this group of elite warriors… I ask… ARE YOU READY TODAY !!!???” “WE ARE READY!!!” “ARE YOU READY FOR VICTORY!!!???” “WE ARE READY!!!”

"THEN LET'S SHOW OUR NEIGHBOURS THE MEANING OF FEAR!!!!"

The sound of war-drums and war-horns increased to the point it became as a heartbeat in each body. Dharmaputra and the commanders got on their horses and slowly started walking towards the gates. As they walked out people showered flowers on the path and on the soldiers. As they approached the gate, they saw Lajwanti and the wives of commanders and captains standing to do last minute war rights and prayers for their husbands. The drums and horns slowly died down as the front row stopped a few feet from the group and the group of women stepped forward. Each started silently reciting an ancient prayer as they held a special platter with auspicious items and a lamp with the undying flame – The Jot. As they prayed, they moved the platter up and down in a gentle circle as if trying to encircle the frame of the person in front of them. Then they moved around the horses sprinkling holy water on the horses and the riders. The riders then bowed down where every lady marked the center of their rider's forehead with the mark of their goddess. As if on que, the drums and the horns slowly started their beats again and the group of ladies stepped aside. Sharp as an arrow all men were… *We have the reason… We have the training… and now… we have the blessings that our wives have asked from our matron goddess.* The column changed shape like the tip of a spear as they approached the gate. First rays of the Sun kissed Dharmaputra on the forehead as he stepped out. Seeing their leader, top commanders and captains, hundreds of soldiers standing outside broke out into excited cheers. The front column slowly swept up hundreds of soldiers off the field in an ordered procession as if a giant piece of dark cloth was being dragged across the land. *…just a week my love… just a week…* □

In two days, the forces reach the outskirts of the city of Bahrauli and set up camp on one side of the field where the war was expected to happen. Dharmaputra looked at his forces readying for tomorrow. *Tomorrow it will start, and, in a few hours, it will be over... how quickly history can change given enough power...* Food tasted different. something filled him with this energy that he was craving for... he wondered if it was something else... *the air... the blessing of gods...* He knew he would win but he was loving the experience.

Next day came too soon. It had always been like that. All forces got ready and lined up in formation on the field. "I would give it to them..." Dharmaputra spoke to his commander as he saw the puny size of the opposing force. At that time, a thought crossed his mind, he asked his commanders if they have companies on the field flanks for any sort of surprise attacks. The commander confirmed. "... well, they are bold... but... just boldness doesn't win battles." He looked to his sides... his commanders ready... he gave the word.

As he thought, in a few hours the fight was over. There were no surprise attacks. He knew now it would be the boring task of taking over the city with as few casualties as possible. To his surprise it took longer than he thought – more than a week but then the city fell. Once the forces established themselves in the city, Dharmaputra started preparations to head back. He would be leaving bulk of his forces behind to keep order but that was part of the plan. A team sent in by Satyachandra was also doing very well as they calmed the public and the local businesses and urged them to settle down. After listening to all the stories about Vajrayudha, the public was already ripe for anyone who would offer a semblance of order. Dharmaputra'a competitive team of administrators coupled with renowned pundits from Varanasi didn't find taking control of the city hard at all.

A few days after that Dharmaputra returns to his palace victorious with the usual fanfare. However now he had nothing exciting to look forward to for a while. He was expecting to have a great time in the war for Baharauli but all that had ended without much effort and all too soon. He felt empty. He wanted to do something exciting. He thought of the next step in Kal's plan. *Kal's plans have been perfect... now I can announce myself independent and the Gyalpo of this country.... My country!!! Yes... that's what I should do next. Gyalpo Mangsung might have the land, but he sure does not have the army to oppose me.* He knew he was right. He had done the math – many times over. This, however, seems to be the only excitement left for Dharmaputra in the next few days. He asked the pundits to find an auspicious date for the announcement and was told about a month from then. Days passed without a problem. That was a problem for Dharmaputra. He didn't have anything to work on. Anything to fight for. One night he retired to his bed bored and tired of inactivity. He found himself looking outside the same window he had heard his men prepare for war. All he heard today was mosquitoes and crickets. *What is the point of being a ruler if you can't even fight a decent war... Bahrauli was barely a fight... not even a week!!! Are people such cowards now??? No, that cannot be!!!*

He sits in silence for a long time thinking if it indeed was true. *Seems like no one enjoys a good fight anymore!!! I wish if there was a way to... to...* and he found himself confused and unable to think further. He thought about what he was just thinking for but found himself unable to even explain it to himself. *Like a dream that one forgets as one tries to remember it...* He knew he had thought about things to be different. *But also, not different in a way... it was so clear a moment ago... only if I knew what that thing was...* For a brief moment, he regretted not studying other things at school. *All these bookish things... argh... what am I thinking... useless thoughts... I am just tired...* He seemed to have nothing else to think about. His mind had given up and his eyes closed. □

The next day starts quieter than expected. He had expected the halls to be busier *even a bit festive???* than yesterday given they were closer to the date when he would announce himself as king. It seemed quite strange, but he couldn't bring himself to ask anyone since he didn't know what exactly to ask for. Everything else seemed to be as expected. Till now administration had been taken care of quite well by his ministers and things had gone quite well. *It's just me... I am bored and am getting impatient... and my council knows how to handle things. They might just be keeping things a bit under the wraps. Until the actual day. That's actually... smart... but boring...ugh!!!* However, as he walked towards his court, it started seeming less and less like it's just him. The court was indeed quieter than yesterday. As he neared the door, he was sure something was wrong. *hell... its quieter than ever... something is wrong...* He hurried in and saw most standing and talking in hushed voices. Everyone bowed as he entered and took the throne. Without even asking, Sahdev stepped forward and presented him a folded royal missive and stepped back. As he looked at Sahdev in surprise, he noticed that everyone was looking at him. *Now I really want to see what's going on!!!* He read the missive.

Dharma, or let me say this formally. Thupo Dharmaputra, as your cousin I have forever lived under your shadow. With me at the helm of your administrative team our lands grew in wealth and prosperity. That said, although, you never even once cared for any of my efforts, I still explained your behavior towards me, as acceptable. This was because in my heart, I understood that we are all children of Buddha. You have clearly shattered that illusion I had since so many years and have confirmed it vehemently with your newfound devotion to the Hindu religion. I have seen that you have stopped paying any attention to the suffering of our Buddhist populace. The people are calling for help and being of the royal lineage who is still true to the spirit of our lands it falls on me to take up this burden. I have stepped up to answer the call of our people and to make you see reason. Consider this as a formal challenge to a duel where I am confident your gods will be powerless in the light of our lands, the light of truth and the light of Buddha. With the support of the people, I declare Doti, Jumla and Kurmanchal no longer under your rule. I instead claim these regions for Gyalpo Mangsung and will report directly to him. If, however, you have the courage to face me in combat, come and claim what you might think is yours. If not, stay where you are – consider yourself forever banished from our ancestral lands and culture.

Tupo of Doti, Jumla and Kurmanchal

Shivaputra

Dharmaputra is on fire. His eyes burning stars. *This rat!!! Even after I gave him all this...* "After all he showed his true colors..." "Sire, our armies are ready to take control back...", said someone. *This insect... !! he will die... he will die like he never imagined... the pain he is going...* "Sire, we can start today and by tomorrow we can..." "NO" The minister bows and steps back as the Thupo stands up shouting. "I will show this this insect what is the meaning of this mistake. I have never interfered with what you do because I trust all of you. He has taken advantage of my trust. Of all our trust. I know our forces can get control of what he thinks he controls in a week. But I want to show him how we treat insects like him." The Thupo looks at his court.

Fuming at his nostrils. "For the crimes against our court and our lands HE WILL DIE!!! HE WILL DIE BY MY VERY OWN HANDS!!! DOES ANYONE… ANYONE OBJECT???" Silence. No one dared. They knew Dharmaputra had the right. Shivaputra had issued the challenge. He has to face the consequences now. "WE LEAVE TONIGHT!!!" Thupo walked out of the court as it fell into a bustle of activity for the upcoming journey.

The journey of a day was completed by the next evening where Thupo settled camp outside Dhoti. It was an awkward evening as armies that were one army a week ago, prepared separately on each of their positions and defenses. On both sides, there were talks about the duel tomorrow. Old veterans recounted how Shivaputra used to be the bigger bully as a kid before Dharmaputra came into his own. Since then, Shivaputra has mostly been an administrator however, he had not completely given up martial arts. Moreover, there was talk about how he was a frequent visitor at the martial school at Sravasti and kept his skills sharp all these years. The thoughts of various types of weapons and different moves that he might expect tomorrow fills Dharmaputra's head as he tries to sleep. As time passes, his thoughts drift into dreams of the day he decided to learn how to fight. □

Distant talk between two people trying to discuss where they should erect the tents reached his ears followed by a guard telling them to keep their voices down. As Dharmaputra opened his eyes his head felt heavy. Lajwanti came in and saw that he was about to wake up. She sat beside him and put the back of her hand on his forehead. "My love, are you feeling ok? You seemed to have the most disturbed sleep last night. You kept tossing and turning and even trying to speak something about Shivaputra in your sleep." She looked at him for a response. Her eyes full of concern. That slight headache seemed to be subsiding as he sat up straight. *Maybe I am getting old... maybe that is the answer to why people are no longer interested in wars... because they are getting old now... just like me...* "Can I have a glass of lemon water? I think it will do good for the slight headache I had a couple of moments ago." Lajwanti got more concerned. Yet again, she checks if Dharmaputra has fever, but it didn't look like that. She called in the maid and asked her to get drink at once. As she left, Dharmaputra started to stand up "My love, you can rest for a day. Your health is the most important thing. I am sure the ministers will be able to run things for the next few days. Anyways, all that is happening is preparation for the ceremony in a week. So, you should just relax for some time." Dharmaputra stood up and walked to the window. He saw preparations going on for his ceremony in various stages. "It's my fault. I had ordered them to make sure things complete on time and they kept working during night as well. I will order them to not work around this area at night. Any celebration isn't worth your health my love.", said Lajwanti. *Indeed, it was the most disturbed sleep. Those dreams ... just my mind showing me my hidden fears...* "I think you are right... I do seem to need a good night sleep." Somewhere inside his forehead a point above his eye pulsed with pain. *...aaaa... arrghh...* He bent down pressing his palm on his eye as Lajwanti rushed towards him. "Oh love, what is wrong." She yelled for the physician to be called and held him from back. "Take rest my love!!! Rest!!!" And the pain was gone. *Like it was never there...* He felt so fresh... *like I just woke up...* He was confused about what was happening... not knowing what would happen. Lajwanti was worried. *What is happening to me...?* He reached out to the side of the bed and sat down. Deep breath. He waited for himself to stabilize. Nothing happened anymore. He looked at his wife. "Cancel the court today. I will just rest."

Resting, however, was new to Dharmaputra. Not only did he feel completely fresh since the pain had gone away but he also was thoroughly bored. Like his head had been washed clean of any straggling thoughts. His mind was completely empty; a completely new feeling for him. He decided to take a walk in the gardens and take lunch there for a change. At that suggestion, Lajwanti ran off pushing everyone to prepare for today's lunch in the garden. That left Dharmaputra sitting and admiring the beauty around him. He saw the tree which he and Shivaputra used to climb and play together. He remembered how his grandfather used to carry him back in his lap. Then, in a distance, he saw someone being blocked by the guards and then handing them over something. One of the guards walked to him and handed him a missive. It was red in color which told him why this couldn't have waited till tomorrow's court. He opens the message as fast as his hands would allow.

Dear brother,

I regret that this message brings ill tidings. Since our victory of Bahrauli, the local population has become very aggressive, and situation has become extremely volatile. Till now it was small crimes that were something that I was able to contain with our forces however, since the last week, it seems, there is an organized resistance coming into picture. There have already been two attacks on the palace that have been warded off. However, many of our soldiers have lost their lives doing that. I am concerned that we might not hold out third attack. I request you to send your forces here as soon as you get this message. If you don't, retaining, Jumla along with Dhoti might become impossible. I have no news from Kurmanchal but situation might be even worse over there. Please send help soon!

Your humble brother

Shivaputra

As he put down the message thinking what to do, he saw the messenger walking towards him with the other guard behind him trying to stop him. He waved the guard to let him come. "Sire," the messenger bowed, "I apologize I have bitter news. Since I started from Jumla a day ago, I have been informed that Ngapo Shivaputra and his family are no more. There was another attack in the palace and now it is under the control of the rebel army. I was also told that most of the passes I used to travel here are also under the control of the enemy army and I was spared just so that I could deliver you this message."

Dharmaputra did not know what to think. His head was still devoid of any thoughts as it was a few minutes ago. He forced himself to bring himself to bear on the problem but couldn't come up with something that he expected to express his, now missing, feelings. Calm as nothing had happened, he spoke. "Who gave you this message?" "A captain of the rebel army, sire." "Did they have any demands?" "Sire, they intend to reclaim Jumla, Dhoti and Kurmanchal as their own. They say that they have blocked all trade going through the area as well and all the northern traders are with them on this." The messenger handed him another small missive. "They have provided the details of how to contact them if you need to open the trade routes again. This is all they have told me." Dharmaputra didn't know what to think as he opened the second missive. At a distance, he saw Lajwanti walking towards him with an entourage of servants carrying various food items behind her. "You may leave." The messenger bowed and retreated. Lajwanti saw the exchange from afar and knew something wasn't right. She rushed to her husband and inquired if something is wrong. Dharmaputra stood up and looked at all the food that was being brought up behind his wife. He felt pity for his wife working so hard. "Oh, my love... I am so sorry. Something urgent has come up that I have to attend to. Our lunch in the garden will have to wait." "But even the physician has told you to take rest!!!" "I know my love. I know. But this is even more important. I promise I will take care of my health." Said Dharmaputra as he started walking towards the court. "Send my lunch there. I will eat properly. Ok??? Don't worry. Everything will be alright." □

Within the next hour an emergency court was in session with most ministers and the council there. However, they knew they wouldn't be of much help here since what was really needed was a strategic assessment of the area and advice around how an attack could be carried out. Since majority of the commanders were still stationed in Bahrauli, such advice seemed to be unavailable. The two main questions debated on and on were weather to launch an all-out assault or scout the areas first. To some, the assault with majority of the force in Bahrauli didn't make sense without knowing points of danger and enemy strongholds. They suggested in scouting the areas first to understand how to formulate the attack to better the chance of success. The other group cautioned against the rebels gaining and establishing more power in the area while any scouting activities were being carried out, in turn endangering the scouts themselves and revealing the plan.

Dharmaputra knew that the dangers mentioned were very real. The longer they wait, the harder the enemy would be to defeat. He also knew that if he withdrew forces from Bahrauli too quickly he would lose it as soon as he had won it. He had to make a play with what he had. He asked for points where the enemy would least expect an attack. He was told a couple of locations, but he was also cautioned that without accurate scouting there was no way to be sure if that information was accurate. Moreover, the reason they were the least defended locations was because they were naturally hard to reach. Some were on cliffs, some required crossing raging rivers while some others required walking through dense swamps and jungle.

Almost unwillingly Dharmaputra decided to send in whatever troops he had to attack the lightly defended points. He proposed, that just like reaching these points is hard for his forces, once claimed, it will be hard to attack, for the enemy as well. Once we have claimed these points, we can use these points as staging areas as well as points where enemy can be attacked from behind the lines to weaken their positions in a frontal attack in the near future. A few commanders are sent to implement this plan.

However, within a week unfortunate news of the companies perishing to accidents or hidden enemy units launching surprise attacks reaches

Dharmaputra. "The locals are with the rebels, sire. They are spying for them. The hilly terrain makes it even slower for our men. Especially since they are not taking the regular paths. With enemy archers deployed on the cliffs, our men are sitting ducks. Sire, sending more men there would be suicide.", said someone from his council. Dharmaputra agreed and nodded. *I know... I would have done the same if I was on the other side... sigh.* "I need to think about this. Let's reconvene tomorrow."

Sitting alone in a pile of maps, wooden pieces to indicate armies, and ledgers showing army strengths, Dharmaputra felt it hard to believe it was the same day when he was sitting in the garden without a worry in the world. His dream to become a Gyalpo seemed a distant hope right now. If he loses Jumla and Dhoti, he would lose control of all the trade routes that bring in all the money he depended on to maintain his forces. All of what he had built would fall in a month or so, when it would be time to pay the bills. He kept thinking but since today morning his head had been an empty vessel. He went to his study and opened the many books on strategy his schools had published but he was not able to find something that could help him with this situation. As night grew darker and the oil lamps dimmed, his eyes and mind gave up on the focus they could muster. He drifted in a world of dreams that smelled like books and had him reading and planning for something important and unknown at the same time. □

Next morning was quiet. Exceptionally quiet. There were orders from commanders to suppress all and any type of noise. It was imperative that Thupo gets a full sleep. Dharmaputra's hand searched for the book he was reading before he could even open his eyes. He couldn't understand how he had gotten on a bed. *Did I walk to my bed last night !!!??? huh!!!* Out of disbelief, he forced open one of his eyes slightly. The books were gone. He wasn't in his study anymore. A tent on what looked like a battlefield. He smelled campfire and morning breeze. His head was heavy like yesterday however, he had no clue why or where he was. *I...ugh... how... where am I...* as he got up, the same pain, he had experienced yesterday shot up somewhere above his eye. He winced and pressed his forehead where it hurt the most. *Its throbbing... arghh...* In a few moments however, it was gone. *Just like yesterday... what is it !!!??? and again... I feel so... fresh!!! How is this possible... is someone drugging me !!!??? it must be!!!* He looked up and saw the heavy cloth of the tent entrance flapping slowly with the morning breeze. As he got up and his eyes saw a missive on a table he seemed to recognize. He picked it up and read it. *Shivaputra's challenge to duel... sigh... so... uhh... this... is real!!!??? Oh my god...* he sat down. He tried to remember his dream. *Such confusion... planning out something and failing every time... ugh... I am glad that was a dream... I... I need to rest... like really rest!!! Once I deal with this insolent fool... I will go on a vacation somewhere.* With a deep breath, he stood up and made himself ready for the day.

Unbeknownst to him, his loyal spymaster had played out the opposite card in the enemy camp. A small unit of suicide assassins had been secretly dispatched in the enemy fort to scare and spread panic around the royal quarters throughout the night. Concerned for his and his family's safety Shivaputra had barely gotten any sleep. Since the challenge was issued by him, he knew, withdrawing at the last minute would mean certain death. Well played brother... well played... he thought as he realized he did not stand a chance to win today in this condition. He knew it could very well be his last day. He only hoped if somehow his family could be spared the wrath of the enemy army. His horse slowly walked out of the castle towards the pavilion. When he looked around, he saw awe, he saw pity and he saw something that told him *"you brought it on yourself... no one can help you now..."*

The horse cleared the gates and walked on the open slope that led to the pavilion with only a few soldiers from the fort garrison behind him. He almost fell off as he woke up when the open and cold air hit him. His breathing was heavy. The inside of his helmet felt so soft. *Or was it the fur on the horse...* He realized he could barely keep his eyes open. *I don't need to keep my eyes open... the horse knows the way... it's going to follow the horse in the front...* a jolt and he sat up straight... *WHY THE HELL DID I DO IT !!!???... why did I fall for Vajrayudha's scheme... he just used me as a pawn... seem like this is what you get for being greedy...* Yawn. He saw his family standing in the crowd. He felt like he was being taken to his execution and his family is going to pay the price of his stupidity.

His eyes opened when the horse stopped. *It wasn't a dream... sigh...* As he got down someone handed him a cup with a smelly drink. "Drink this... it will take away the sleep." The cup was hot to touch and whatever was in it smelled nasty even from far. The smell itself caused his eyes to open and water. *Argh... what in the hell is this...* He looked at the person who handed him the cup. He also knew he needed it... No one spoke a word. *You want to die...*

*be my guest...* is what he heard in his mind. He closed his eyes and held his breath as he pushed the caustic mixture down his throat. "Give it some time to settle." Said a voice behind him as he felt something hit him from inside. His eyes opened wide, and he felt heat on his ears and his face.

Dharmaputra was already standing in the pavilion looking down at him. Shivaputra was breathing heavy now. His eyes focused on this man in front of him. *It's the same bony kid I used to beat the crap out of... it's going to be the same this time...* He started walking towards him and looked down for a second to see where he was going. He realized how far he was from the pavilion and the average sized man he thought standing a few yards away is standing much farther. *How is he... so... big... it cannot be... it must be the sleep... or this thing I just had...* He tightly closed his eyes, shook his head, and straightened himself as he walked. *Yea.. not so big... a bit... maybe... but not that much...* Heavy breaths followed as he entered the pavilion. As he bent down to get in, he felt the caustic gas from his stomach rise and sting his eyes.

Everyone knew the rules. Yet, someone read the

rules loudly to the audience. The choice of weapon was left to the combatants. It would go on until either one side accepts defeat or the other side is the only one left – a fight till death. Both warriors were told to go on opposite sides of the pavilion and chose their weapons. Shivaputra chose a two-handed axe. He was known for using his strength and weight of the axe to swing it in unexpected moves. Dharmaputra picked up a Gada – a heavy all metal mace with a massive sphere on one end. Shivaputra knew a single blow to his body with that could turn it to a pulp. Now the warriors came in front of each other and waited for the bell.

Shivaputra could see now how much he has misjudged Dharmaputra's physique. He cursed for all the time he kept working in his office never really attending or meeting Dharmaputra to get a fair idea about his built. He tried to get an idea of his opponent's mindset but gave up soon when he found Dharmaputra quite calm and himself too tired already. He knew that Dharmaputra has mostly been working on his strength and hence his choice of weapon. *I would have to see how nimble he is when the fight starts. With his weapon, probably not much. I only have to outmaneuver him and land one shot at him and this should be over.* Dharmaputra had been briefed that his opponent might not be in his best shape today (although he wasn't clearly told the reason). He mostly studied Shivaputra's stance and physical bearing that might help him understand his moves.

The bell went off and the fight started. The crowd watched with their breaths held as the heavy weapons clashed with each other. Dharmaputra seemed to mostly be defending Shivaputra's blows and didn't seem like he was attacking. *He must be thinking of surprising me...* thought Shivaputra as he ducked below to swing his axe close to ground. Dharmaputra jumped, did a spin, and kicked him on his face and landed upright.

Shivaputra on the other hand almost lost his weapon while he fell back. At once Dharmaputra went on an offensive and caused Shivaputra to roll across the ground to avoid the heavy blows that caused round holes to form where he had been a few moments ago. He managed to hit at Dharmaputra's leg causing him to lose balance and giving himself precious few moments to get back on his feet. *I see this is how you are going to do this...* and then that mix hit him. Almost blinding him. Something in his stomach hadn't agreed with all the rolling around and jumping up on his feet so quickly. His eyes wouldn't open. He knew he had... At once something hit his stomach so hard it broke his ribcage and seemed to knock off the back of his spine. At once his mouth filled with what felt like the insides of his body and blood. Instinct caused him to keep his mouth closed but the pressure got too much, too fast. He vomited out what looked like his internal viscera that still seemed to be attached to somewhere inside his body. He fell on his side trying to take a breath. Along with intense pain in his chest, he felt like drowning. His mouth seemed to be stuffed with his insides and nose filled with blood. He knew he wasn't going to come out of this alive. He hadn't been able to get a single shot. *All because of this trickery the night before... he couldn't afford to duel him with a straight mind.* Thoughts of his grandfather saving this bony kid whenever he couldn't defend himself crossed his mind. *I hate you... every fight you have had ... you have won because of some unfair advantage...* His thoughts were getting clouded. He could barely make up from down.

He saw his opponent's feet a few steps from him and tried to judge where he could be. Dharmaputra looked at the crowd around him with arms wide open as they cheered for him. *I will die... but you will not win...* With a last effort he swung his axe where he thought his opponent might be. The axe slipped from his hand came down on the other side of the pavilion. It had blood on the blade. Dharmaputra was caught unawares as the blade sliced open a large gash on his stomach. As his eyes closed, Shivaputra saw the gada hit the ground followed by a pair of knees. *You lose...* he thought. At the same time his body went in convulsions due to lack of air. Biting on his own viscera in his mouth caused even more internal pain and intensified the convulsions.

Two teams of physicians rushed towards the combatants but the one for Shivaputra didn't know where to start from. The other group lifted Dharmaputra and rushed him out of the pavilion to the camp to take care of his bleeding scar. Later, Shivaputra was announced dead and Dharmaputra the victor. However, the crowd didn't seem to agree with the decision but dispersed when the soldiers were brought in. □

Later lying in another tent where a group of physicians were treating him, Dharmaputra regained consciousness. He was told of the result of the duel. A small smile crossed Dharmaputra's lips. *That fool... and he thought he could best me... what was he even thinking...* As he tried to sit up a sharp pain caused him to wince in pain and fall back. The head of the physicians rushed to him and told him that he has suffered serious injury to his stomach, and they are trying to treat him as much as they can. He, however, needs to be on complete rest until told otherwise. They have, in the meantime cancelled any plans to go back to his palace. "Sire, we have informed Lady Lajwanti as well as your personal physician. They will be here in a day or two. "Until then, kindly relax and let us take care of you." Doing just that didn't seem to be that hard for Dharmaputra, who kept on moving in and out of consciousness as time passed. He completely lost track of time or place. Whenever his eyes would open, he would see different things or people. He saw Lajwanti sitting next to him at night and at another time he saw Madhuracharya mixing something and feeding him with it and yet another time he found that he has been shifted into some sort of a room.

Pain coupled with heat caused him to open his eyes. He found Madhuracharya removing his bandages and applying a heated salve on his stomach. "How is it?" he asked. The physician did not answer. He was surprised he was tired of talking already. He could barely talk. "How long has it been?" "About a month." *A month!!!* His voice failed his emotions. "Where am I? Tell me, is this getting better? Tell me the truth!!!" Madhuracharya looked at him. "You are in your palace. Your scar. It's not as bad when you got it. But it hasn't gotten better since." *What does he mean by that...???* He looked at the physician to answer but he did not respond. When his eyes opened again, he found the physician preparing something in the corner of the room. He was feeling a bit better. He used his fingernails to knock on the bed to catch the physician's attention. Madhuracharya came and sat by his side. "What do you mean by that?", Dharmaputra asked. "What do I mean by what?" "What you said... it hasn't gotten better since..." Silence... "...my scar... you said, it hasn't gotten better since..." "oh.. that was a week ago !!!" *a week ago!!!* "You should be feeling a bit better now, don't you?" Dharmaputra nodded in agreement. "Your scar... its quite deep. And it seemed that Shivaputra's axe was laced with something that is making your scar unable to heal. I was expecting you to be walking by now. But instead, I am still struggling for the scar to heal. That is why I have also started working on making sure that you feel invigorated in your body even while the scar is still healing. Maybe once your body has enough strength, it can start curing the scar by itself." Dharmaputra raises his head to look at his stomach. He sees a mess of scabbed tissue and pus starting from the bottom left of his chest and following diagonally down. *This is quite deep...* "And if it does not heal itself?" he looks in the physician's eyes. Madhuracharya turns his gaze downwards towards his scar for some time and then looks back at him. "Let me talk to my colleagues. Maybe they know of some other methods that we can try." *Yes... try something... go talk...* Dharmaputra is too tired. He nods. His eyes close. □

As consciousness comes back to Dharmaputra, he finds his neck is stiff. *It's all the sleeping on this for weeks...* he tries to move but finds that his head is on a hard surface. *I am not on a bed...* The pain on his stomach is gone. *I hope this is good...* His eyes open and he sees crumpled pages of some military strategy book in front of his eyes. He lifts his head to find himself in his study. *What is happening to me...?* He lifts his shirt again to confirm there is no scar present. For a few moments, he rubs his stomach and tries to feel how good not being injured feels. At once, that pain... he knows it... *do I??? is this real... this should go away if I do this...* he brings his hand and presses it against his forehead. In a few moments, the pain is gone. His head clear and mind fresh. *What is happening ... I thought this was a dream!!! Maybe it is... maybe I am in a dream...* He tries to tap on his stomach in anticipation of pain... *nothing... maybe if I sleep again, I will wake up from this dream...* but sleep never comes. Dharmaputra is awake as an owl. He tries various things such as shaking his head violently to spinning in circles to standing on his hands upside down to somersaulting on the ground multiple times... *something might tire me to sleep...* but every time he would open his eyes just as awake as he was when he started. He sat down on the ground, now sweating from all this activity. *I must be going mad... I am jumping up and down to become a dying man from my dream!!! What the hell... instead I should have been focusing on continuing my work from last night... I think, all this stupidity about that dream is only because I want to run away from this situation...* His eyes fall on the board in front of him.

He realizes that he didn't have any men left. None he could spare. *I cannot lose the North!!! I need to think about that differently...* He gets up and sits on the chair. *Ok...let me think... these rebels... what do they even want... why do they even exist... they exist because of me... because they think I am not thinking about the Buddhists. They think I am only thinking about the Hindus. You know what... when I think about it... looking at what has been happening, they could actually think that... they... they are not entirely wrong!!!* Dharmaputra feels sad for his actions and for the Buddhists as he sits in silence and thinks about what he has been doing since the last many months. He couldn't shake off the feeling that he has betrayed his religion... *my true religion... I ... I totally forgot... sigh...* he sits silently looking at the ground thinking what he could have done to prevent this.

His mind races to trace back the root cause that started the chain of problems facing the area as a thought strikes him. *Could it work!!!??? It is the right thing to do anyways... it might make things harder in the South... it will... most surely... but I can't afford to lose the North... if I can't pay the bills, I will lose the South anyways.* He curses the gods under breath. *Arghh...* Silence and heavy breathing follow. *Its Karma. This is punishment for what I did...* His eyes trace the patten on the floor as his mind raced to conclude what he already knew. *I need to go back!!! I am a Buddhist ... I need to repent... and I need to let my people know that I am paying my due. I need to show them that I am doing right by them. They need to know they can trust me. They have done that over all these years... all this change of religion is too much for everyone!!! They just can't take it anymore...* Silence. His eyes settle. Trying to understand what he just thought. Questioning himself. *Really??? Are you really thinking of changing your religion again!!!??? Are you sure that is what you are thinking???* His eyes fell on the board again and he counted the companies he had left. He looked at the books in front of him. All full of how to arrange and deploy armies in various formations but none about what to do when you don't have enough armies in the first place. With his armies in North rebelling, his remaining forces would be spread too thin even if he applied all of it for this purpose.

For the first time in his life, he felt he should have paid more attention in other areas during his schooling. All he knew was war; and nothing else. *Shivaputra is gone… I haven't seen Kal for last many days as well.* As he sits in silence thinking over his plan over and over, he realizes there is no other way. His only chance is to personally go North and meet with the rebel captains. But before he does so, he would have to publicly revert back to Buddhism again. *That is the only way!!! That is the only way the rebels will even talk to me!!!* He walks to the window and looks to the silence outside and imagines the chaos his decision will cause tomorrow morning. All his generals guarding Bahrauli and the Southern borders. It will be hard for them to contain the unrest. *Hard… but not impossible… that is why I am leaving all of them here… that is why I am not moving them. No, it shouldn't be too hard for them. Maybe unexpected…. But not hard…* As he takes a deep breath, the cool night air rushes in his body and seems to quell a fire that had been raging inside him. At once he feels tired and sleepy. He consoles himself as he walks back to his bedroom. *This is the only way. After some time, things would be alright.* □

The next day, the court starts with a somber mood. Dharmaputra asks and waits for any of his ministers to provide an alternative plan to resolve the situation but all he gets is silence and downward stares. *These good for nothing ministers!!! I should fire them as they stand!!!* Once Dharmaputra was sure he had the attention of everyone in the room he addressed the court. "It's my fault. It's my fault that I abandoned our people. I failed to be the example I wished to become for our people...." Everyone looked at him expectantly but unsure of where he was going. "The gods have punished me for this. We all know what it is, and I will be the first one to say it. Its Karma. Its Karma and Buddha is punishing me for my deeds." He could see the court brake out in hushed murmurs.

He looked in each of his minister's eyes as he made the next statement. "You all know what needs to be done. I need to repent for my sins. Sins against my brothers and sisters in North." Dharmaputra wanted to break the news as softly as possible, but he knew it was impossible to do that. "I have learned much in my study of all the Hindu scriptures. My broad studies have taught me the importance of perseverance and devotion. I have realized that I need to continue walking the path I was born to walk. The path I had deserted some time ago." The court was silent. "In this life, I was born a Buddhist and some time ago, I had left that path. This has given me wisdom but also shown me the wrong in my doings that I need to correct. This difficult time has made me realize the folly of my decisions and helped me see reason. I have decided, from today onwards, I will be a Buddhist again." Pandemonium seemed to have erupted across the hall. Dharmaputra was not sure if people were talking to him or yelling at each other.

He waited for the noise to come down to where he could start speaking again. "That is not all." Silence fell back. "I will personally go and meet the rebel armies in the North. In fact, I should not call them rebels. They are my brothers and sisters who have been in pain and are calling out for help." One of the ministers stepped forward to object, but Dharmaputra stopped him with a wave. "I know you are concerned about my safety, but I assure you that I will be safe. I will talk to them and try to figure out a solution to this situation and their problems. I hope to look forward to your support in the days going forward." With that Dharmaputra looked at his council and the rest of the court. *Surprised... uneasy... unsure... I would need to act quickly... Buddha help me!!!* "Minister, prepare the men. We leave tomorrow." □

Although the ministers try to plan for a safe route, Dharmaputra urges and encourages the most straightforward route to the areas controlled by the rebels. Fast riders are sent in advance carrying the news of the Thupo's return to Buddhism as well as his journey to talk to the captains. Against all odds, the plan seems to be working. Only a few know the details of the distribution of his armies in the South and hence assume that a much bigger army might be following Thupo's company. The captains agree to meet him and discuss their demands. *This is progress... Oh Buddha... please keep your blessing on me and I will correct all my sins ... I promise...*

Dharmaputra meets with multiple captains from various areas; each has a different ask specific to his own area. Some even want to control territories and routes claimed by other captains. The demands are many and by the end of two days Dharmaputra has a stack of papers listing asks ranging from to territorial to specific resources to specific percentages in trades for various items on the trade routes. Dharmaputra let's the captains know that he needs to sort out what he can agree to in the next two days and mostly receives a fairly positive response from them. *They all seemed happy with me becoming Buddhist, but they want assurances. They can't trust me right now. I can't blame them... I wouldn't trust me right now!!! However, they are not united... that is exactly what I needed... I can play them against each other!!! The ministers should be looking at the asks tonight and tomorrow. I am sure we can figure out something reasonable...*

He realizes how much tired, all this "mind work" has made him and as he lays down in his bed, he takes a deep breath. A small smile touches his lips as his eyes close. *It's working... tomorrow will be good!!!* □

Dharmaputra had a busy sleep that night. The excitement of a solution coupled with the anxiety of how the rebel forces would respond had him dreaming a cacophony of dreams that didn't make sense. Even when sleeping he knew he had to get up, but he kept his eyes shut so that he is well rested tomorrow. As hours passed, the discomfort of lying still was getting too much to bear. He did not know if it was just his dreams or if he was feeling cramps all over his body due to lying down for so long. He couldn't bear it any longer and decided to wake up. The pain did not go away though. In fact, he realized he couldn't even get up.

He found himself in a familiar room... with a familiar person... tending to a familiar wound. *Looks like Shivaputra had indeed won...* He saw the thick scab on his lower chest covered by thick smelly cloth. He pressed it with a finger, and it was still moist. As he pressed more, he felt a shooting pain in his stomach, and he almost cried out. Madhuracharya rushed towards him, pulled his hand away from his wound and adjusted the bandages again. *Sigh... how long...* "Madhuracharya... is this... curable?" The physician was silent, hesitant, his eyes twitching about. *He had to ask his colleagues...* "Did you ask your colleagues?" The physician nodded. "What did they say?" Madhuracharya looked him in the eye for a moment and then turned his gaze downwards. *What does he mean!!!??? "What do you mean???" argh... this pain...* "Is there no cure for this???" After a few moments the physician looked up. "Sire, there is one, but I do not know if it will work. It's been a family secret of one of my colleagues. His family has never discussed it publicly and hence there is no proof if it works or not. I am also a bit hesitant about it since it mostly seems some magic hocus-pocus and not really any real medicine that I have experience with. I am not sure if it will heal you or make it even worse." *So... there is something...* "Well, is it one of your colleagues who told you about it?" "Yes, my sire." "And this colleague of yours... how is his standing in your field?" "He is another renowned physician in the service of another king sire. However, he has claimed that he has never used this technique on anyone outside his own family. Not even on the king he serves." Silence. *Hummm... that is confusing indeed... taking this treatment is pretty much a gamble...* The physician spoke again "Well, in his defense he has added that he has also not had the occasion to use it in his career till now." *...ok...*

"well, if he had the occasion to use it, would he be confidant to use it?" "Only within his family and only with the express permission of the one being treated and only as a last resort" *...argh... this does not inspire confidence at all!!! Sigh...* "Madhuracharya, tell me... be honest..." The physician looked at him. "Is there another way?" The physician was quiet for a long time. "Sire, time is a great healer. There is no harm in waiting." *... so, he doesn't know anything else...* "Ok, tell me what is this treatment? I want to understand why you are so concerned about it." "Sire, I don't know how to describe it. From my point of view, it's quite simple actually. I will prepare a special paste and rub it on your wound. The patient... you... need to stay in your bed for half a day and then go to a place I can mark on the map. Apparently, the paste is supposed to expand your soul in very specific ways. Once you reach the spot you need to be alone and without any clothes. His words were – 'as you were born' and with the power of the paste, you are to find the voice of God!! Once you are able to find that voice, it should be able to heal you." Madhuracharya had a disgusted expression on his face. *Well... that doesn't sound that bad... what if it actually works???!!!* "I know what you are thinking sire. It's not hard to do in general, but in your condition going all alone in the snow without any clothes... and for how long will you stay there searching for this 'Voice of God!!!'??? Especially without anyone with you or knowing about your exact whereabouts!!! Its madness!!!"

Dharmaputra felt unable to shake his eyes off the physician's stare that was all logic and sense. "Well... you are right... this is madness." *Sigh... what was I thinking... he is right...* Madhuracharya got off the side of the bed and turned towards the corner of the room where he was boiling some herbs. *Argh... these cramps...* laying down for weeks... *months???...* seemed to have taken a toll on the Thupo's back. The soft mattress felt like a bed of rocks. Even the seams of his clothes burned and cut into his skin as rough jute rope would. *Every breath is a fight here... argh...* he winced in pain as he adjusted his body. *I... I can't do this anymore... what do I have to lose... it's not like I am not in pain here... plus if this works, I can get back to Varanasi once for all... now that it is so close to my grasp!!! And if it doesn't work... well... I can always just come back from wherever I need to go... I am too close to give up now... if I give up now... all this work I put in... changing religion... bribing people.... And putting all these months of my life would be for nothing... I am too close now... and I am getting tired of this bed... and this stupid physician who has given up on me already... I am going...* "Madhuracharya. Prepare the treatment. There is risk but I want to get well now. I've had enough." The physician turned back amid his stride surprised at the sudden change of heart. "Sire!!! but..." "No, do as I say." He looked down. "Sire, would you please allow me to call the queen to attendance to discuss this further." "Physician! Do as you are commanded." "As you wish my liege. However, I would still need the queen to be here to hold you down in case you experience any pain or discomfort for half of the day when you are on the bed with the paste." "Do what you need to." The physician bows and rushes out. □

The paste smells absolutely atrocious. All staff in the castle have to resort to covering their nose and mouths with heavy cloth while its prepared and administered to the Thupo. The news of this weird treatment spreads quickly as marshals are told about leaving the Thupo alone after a specific point in his journey and to ensure no one follows him.

The paste takes some time to start working but as soon as it does, its effects are clear. Dharmaputra goes from being cold to sweating profusely. Lajwanti is concerned and asks him repeatedly if he is feeling ok to go on this journey. "My love... I am worried for you... you are taking this treatment against the advice of the physician... this is very risky my love..." Dhaarmaputra keeps looking somewhere beyond the roof of the room. "Ah my girl... my lovely, lovely girl... don't be scared... I am already feeling better than ever... I already hear faint whispers in distance... I know what I need to do Laj... Once I go there... I will be ok..." He seems to listen to something afar... "no... better than ok... don't worry my love... have faith ... I hear the whispers from God!!!" *Its working!!! Its working!!!... ah... I love this...* He closes his eyes with a smile, "Wake me up when it's time to leave." □

*It's just been a few moments... I thought I had to wait half a day...* Eyes still closed; Dharmaputra slowly comes back to the waking world surprised at how well the paste is working. *This was the best sleep I've had in days... I will let Madhuracharya know that he needs to learn from this friend of his...* He cannot help but smile at how well things are going and *how he will be well soon... ah... The pain seems to have gone already... now its just a matter of healing the scar... I love it... I love it...* The hand trying to wake him up felt a bit heavier than his wife's. *Who is this...?* He opened his eyes and found a set of eyes looking down at him.

*Where am I...* At the back of this person, he saw his room where he was staying while negotiating with the rebel captains. *Am I in a dream!!!??? How is this happening!!!???* He saw two eyes full of rage and face hidden behind the cloth mask coming down from the turban. *The mask of an assassin!!!* Instantaneously his smile turned into dread. He tried to yell but no voice came out. *This has to be a dream... this should be the paste... I need to wake myself up... I know these eyes!!! Is he one of the rebel captains??? But why would they want to kill me.... They all seemed so happy yesterday...* At once, he felt the sharp cold point of a dagger on his chest. *I need to wake up... I just need to shake myself to get up...* He tried to move but the weight of the attacker kept him pinned. The movement caused the cloth covering the face to lose its grip from somewhere and fall down. *KAL!!!!* A sudden force of sadness hit him. All he could do is to ask him *WHY!!!????* His eyes would have to do the talking today.

"There is no point in trying to move. The toxin should paralyze you in a few moments. You will, however, feel the full pain of this blade going into your chest." Suddenly he found himself unable to move his lower body. All he could do is watch as his breathing became heavy. "After all I did to help you to become what you are, you have the audacity to disgrace the Hindu religion!!! All this time I tried to show you the way and as soon as you found yourself in a small pickle you showed your true colors. You are not worthy of being a Hindu!!! It was me who made you move and pollute our sacred religion and hence it is my responsibility to clean up this filth. I have ensured Satyachandra will give King Vajrayudha complete control over all your lands. The whole Hindu world will see to it. Moreover, as we speak, my colleagues are expunging our pristine lands of any trace of your family as well. Possibly in ways much like what is happening to you or much more painful ways even. We will burn you out of existence!!! Say your last prayers Dharmaputra but know they won't be answered since there is no God that is looking after you."

Everything was happening too fast. Dharmaputra tried to speak but could not even move his lips. His eyes widened as he felt the cold of the blade turn into sharp sting and intense pressure as it slowly dug deeper in his chest. Kal's voice seemed to be booming in his ears now, "PRAISE GODDESS KALI!!! PRAISE GODDESS KALI!!!". Kal marked his forehead with the blood spraying out of his chest. The knife hilt was on his chest now and he could feel its tip somewhere inside him at his spine!!! Dharmaputra's world turned into colors, and he remembered something. *This is just a dream... I know... this is a dream... it's just that paste... I know... how funny it is that something so simple as a medicine could cause such horrible dreams...* As his eyes closed, he smirked while he felt a cold blade on his neck. □

*What a dream...hah... time to go...* as his eyes opened, he found himself taking another step forward in the snow. *Oh... I am already here!!! Well... in that case it's definitely this medicine!!! I don't even remember how I came here or where this place is...!!!* He looked down and found that there was blood on the snow. *That is a lot of blood!!! Sigh...* He was feeling sleepy... *Maybe Madhuracharya was right... I should sit somewhere... O voice of God... just wait for a few moments while I rest...* The ground where his blood had melted the snow seemed warmer on his skin and he liked it. *I need some more blood here ... then I can rest my hand in its warmth here as well...*

His eyes opened and he saw a blurry figure in front of him. *Is this God...???* "Praise to the God!!! Praise to the God!!! I have come as you asked. Please bless.... cure..." He was too tired to speak. With his neck barely supporting his head he saw the figure approach him. *Who is this... I know these clothes...* The figure slapped him so hard he almost fell on his side. Then he heard a laugh he recognized. *Madhuracharya...!!! It cannot be...* He tried to look up but failed... his strength failed to keep his torso straight against the tree and he felt his head hit the ground. Everything became sideways.

"You fool... you thought I couldn't cure a simple cut!!! With you gone, Maharaja Vajrayudha would finally be able to purify these lands you had been rotting all these years. What did you think when you hired me as your physician?? That me, a Hindu Brahmin of the highest level would stoop so low as to serve you!!! If nothing else, your house would remember how foolish their leader was in touching our holy lands by pretending to change their religion and how he died with dung all over his body. In a short time, they will find you dead at the hand of some untested cure that everyone and including me..." he laughed, "warned you against. Your children would be executed to make sure your line does not continue. Your wife would be sold in some un-named market as a slave. My mission has been fulfilled. Good riddance!!! Long live Maharaja Vajrayudha!!!", and he walked away. Enraged, Dharmaputra tried to yell but only coughed blood. There was only pain, hatred and sleepiness in Dharmaputra's dying mind. *How could I not see... what did I miss...* Sitting silently, he gulped blood and snot... a sharp sting of cold made him think something... *this could be another dream as well...*

*could this be… another damn dream ??? please be…*

*I need to wake up… □*

*What was I thinking…!!!* As his eyes open, he sees his commanders ready for his word. The attack for Bahrauli was about to begin and everyone was at the edge of their breath. With a single word, a tsunami of warriors rushes towards the enemy ranks. Dharmaputra watches as the fight is over within hours. All this time he could not shake off the feeling of having the strangest thoughts *or were they dreams??? But when did I dream them!!!??? This is so confusing…*

It had turned out many soldiers had defected from enemy ranks as they had supported Dharmaputra's control of the region and see his victory as the liberation of Hindus. Dharmaputra's forces don't find any problems establishing control in the city, especially after the defected soldiers come forward with request to join Dharmaputra in maintaining order. *Its time now!!! Time to show Mangsung who is the real ruler here.* Dharmaputra calls a secret meeting of his council and orders them to start preparing for a ceremony when he will declare himself Gyalpo. "I want this to be their next assignment once our forces have recuperated and rested. This will be their crowing hour. To win their lands independence. To make their country a kingdom!!!" *Nothing could make a soldier more proud!!!*

The next day after the court he asks Minister Sahdev to stay back. "What can I do for my liege." "Respected minister, I have to ask you something that might seem really weird but believe me I have serious reasons to ask this." Sahdev gives him a concerned look. "Minister, I don't want to worry the queen without any reason, but have I been possibly behaving strangely in court or outside? Is there any news, or even any rumor of any such thing?" Sahdev is really confused, "Sire, we all know how you find the affairs of the court boring, and your specialty is the area of martial arts. We don't mind if we sometimes find you resting while we sort out the mundane everyday affairs in the court hall. Other than that, I am quite confident that sire is has been quite capable without an exception." *Hmm.... well... could it all really been just a thought... I could remember all that so clearly... how... oh... just thinking about all that makes me so tired... maybe that is what it is... I am getting old... I probably need to relax a bit more...* He notices Sahdev still standing expecting him to say something. "Thank you minister. I request you to please keep this conversation to yourself. I do not want to worry the queen without reason." "You have my word sire!" "Thank you. How goes the preparation for our next attack?" "From my point of view, you don't need to worry about a thing. The spymaster has told me that Mangsung's armies are in no shape to fight for his claim. We control most of the trade in the lands and although I don't like to boast, we can even go in this fight just using hired armies if we needed to!!! Your highness has executed his moves wisely and at the most appropriate moment!!! I am no military expert, however even I can see that this should be an easy victory!!!" With a smile Dharmaputra asks the minister to leave. *You are right Sahdev... and I cannot wait to become a Gyalpo!!!*

The next day the envoy of trade merchants of the Bahrauli comes to his court and state that he has been able to unite a large part of the trade routes and has been able to make them safe for trade. This according to envoy's head trader, "has won him their appreciation and they have some gifts for him." They present him with many material gifts however the head trader tells him that he has been informed of the location where the mystical creature that Dharmaputra has tried to hunt before has been seen. The head trader also wants to present this location directly to Dharmaputra so that he and he alone can reach the creature before anyone else. He hands him a map marked with a location. *Oh, what happy news is this!!! I shall start for this hunt tomorrow morning itself... before the creature changes its location!!!*

The next day he selects his closest captains and starts for the hunt that is supposed to take two days. He also takes his trusted dog, Shera, with him. He knows that Shera will be able to pick up on any odd scent trails in the area. When they reach the area, he asks everyone to spread out and give the signal when they spot the creature. Almost immediately Shera catches sent of a trail and the Dharmaputra tries to walk behind him as fast as he could. That said, he intentionally tries to keep his feet very soft on the ground to reduce any sort of noises that could alert the creature. Then almost unexpectantly he reaches an opening and sees Shera was right. He sees the mystical creature in all its glory. It's the golden stag from all the tales he has heard. Its huge, about twice his own height with his huge antlers rising even higher than that. Although the forest was quite dark, the creature seems to be bathed in golden light from somewhere.

Dharmaputra knows he needs to get closer to be able to hit it with an arrow. However, he has to be extremely careful and deliberate to make sure he remains unseen. He silently pulls his bow forward and knocks an arrow. The body of the bow bends and stresses as he silently pulls the back the bowstring. An almost inaudible creek in his bow catches his attention. His eyes dart to the point from where the sound could have come from but almost instantaneously return back on his target. He finds he is not the only one who has heard the sound. The creature looking at him. His eyes meet the stag's eyes while his body is frozen still. He is still a few steps away to take the shot. On his signal Shera makes a run for the animal. The stag starts to turn back, and Dharmaputra engages in a sprint to cover these few steps as soon as possible. He runs with his eyes are still on his target and his body is still in the same posture of knocked bow ready to let the arrow go in a moment. He knows he will only get one shot and he wants to make it count. One more step and he would let the arrow go. In his mind he makes ready to bend on his knees as soon as he would land and launch the arrow – his focus still on the target. However, as his foot touches on the ground it doesn't stop as it should have. He sees the ground level getting higher and his target hiding behind this rising horizon. Instantly he notices the fake grass collapsing in with him in a hole. He can do nothing as he sees himself heading towards a bed of spikes at the bottom of the pit. His eyes close in anticipation of the pain. Multiple lightning bolts strike his body instantaneously. He cannot yell as his jaw is lodged between different spikes coming out of his mouth. He feels a cold sensation from the back of his neck to the center of his forehead as his skull is supported by a spike going through one end and stopping short of coming out of the other.

As his eyes close, he sees a blurry figure appear on the edge of the pit and look down. Dharmaputra squints to focus his vision but his eyes fail to cooperate. As his eyes close, he hears voices one of which sounds familiar. "No, it's done! Let's go home…" "Laj, this man has made you suffer so much… made your kids suffer so much… in the last two years how many times have you even seen him?

Maybe you might be ok, but do you think your kids will ever be able to forgive their father?" *Laj!!! With whom??? ...ah... so... tiring...* Silence. It is getting harder to hear for Dharmaputra. "If not to anyone else, you owe it to your children to look him in the eye and tell him that he deserves this. If you don't do it now, you will regret it all your life..." Dharmaputra tries again and this time his eyes come into focus. He sees it was Vajrayudha who was looking down at him. Now another shape comes into his view. *Laj...* he tries to speak but his muscles don't move. He sees the love of his life crying. "Tell him what he needs to hear dear... tell him!!!" *This... rascal.... how... dare...* it is getting harder to breath... *what lies have you been feeding her...* Then his wife speaks. "What did we not do for you??? I... Loved you... more than myself..." *Sigh... but I have loved you!!!* He saw Vajrayudha take his sobbing wife into his arms and console her. From a corner he sees Vajrayudha smirk back at him. *THIS BASTARD!!!* Dharmaputra couldn't contain his rage. His body shook as he tried to sit up. At once something gave under him and he fell even more, driving even more things into his body and pushing those already inside even deeper. He felt his skull crack from inside and something rip the skin of his forehead. His rage only grew as he felt his body grow numb. *I SHOULD...* he wasn't sure if he was imagining, seeing or hearing things... *KILL HIM!!! Pain everywhere... suffocation... Is this... Is this another dream???!!! This has to be a dream. argh... sigh... I will wake up soon.* ∎

# ABOUT THE AUTHOR

Rupendra Dhillon born in New Delhi, India, observed, at a very early age, his father burning the midnight oil on his trusty writing pad and Remington typewriter.

Now settled in the rural outskirts of Toronto, Canada, with his wife and two dogs, he has taken up a hobby very similar to his father's. His aim is to tell stories that grab the reader's attention and pack an emotional punch.

To get in touch with him and for updates about his upcoming work, visit rupendradhillon.com.

www.ingramcontent.com/pod-product-compliance
Lightning Source LLC
Chambersburg PA
CBHW051758050726
47598CB00006B/2338